DRAGON FEVER

MASTERS OF THE FLAME

MATING FEVER

ELSA JADE

Also by Elsa Jade

Mating Season:
Wolves of Angels Rest

Hero
Joker
Rogue
Warrior
Lost Wolf
Ghost Wolf
Cry Wolf
Fighter
Wish Upon a Werewolf

Mating Fever:
Masters of the Flame

Dragon Fever
Dragon Fate
Dragon Fall

Intergalactic Dating Agency:
Big Sky Alien Mail Order Brides

Alpha Star
Red Shift
Dark Matter

CHAPTER ONE

"Ladies, step into the Keep"—with the touch of a button, the doorman flung open the wide double doors into the casino—"and enter a world of fabulous treasure and mystery."

On the verge of entering, Piper Ramirez hesitated. The only mystery was what on earth she was doing at this crazy place.

Ahead of her, the gaping hallway was pitch-black except for crystal pendants dangling from above like menacing teeth, then sconces in the stone walls flared to life. Piper bit back a gasp. The flames couldn't be real. And if they were, no way would she stay in a place with such a fire hazard.

She glanced uncertainly at her friends. Anjali had directed the bellboys to their bags and was standing on the sidewalk with her red head tipped back, staring up at the façade.

Though the Keep was on the very edge of Vegas city limits, it rivaled anything on the Strip for sheer size, so Piper didn't blame Anj for gawking. Meanwhile, Esme was just getting out of the limo, zipping her Hermes purse. She'd probably tipped the driver despite the fact the man was employed by Esme's stinkin'-rich fiancé to squire them around on their last long weekend as free women.

Free. Even though Esme was the one getting married, it felt to Piper as if all three of them were trapped in ways that just a few years ago they swore they'd never allow. Esme was letting her wealthy family guilt her into marrying one of their even wealthier business associates. Anjali was slaving at her nutty uncle's head shop instead of pursuing her art.

Only Piper was sticking to her post-college game plan: turn her chemical engineering degree into a good, steady job, and never again let anyone tell her what she could or couldn't be.

But even she felt like she wasn't quite...there. Like she was still missing something. And her edginess was making her all kinds of confused when she was supposed to be the laid-back one in their friendship trio.

Now this was her last chance to remind her friends of the promises they'd made—not to each other or anyone else, but to themselves.

First order of business—Piper glanced sidelong at Anjali who had finally stepped up beside her in the casino doorway—get an ally.

"The Keep keeps it all," Anjali murmured. "What kind of casino reminds its marks that the house always wins the 'fabulous treasure'?"

"An honest one?" Piper mused. "Or one that knows that people always think the rules don't apply to them."

Anjali smirked at her in agreement. Anj might've been dragged back into her old haunts when her uncle needed someone to watch his shop, but at least she was wearing the braided ring with the inset fire opal she'd designed back in their first year of living together. So she must still remember some of those dreams they'd shared over raw cookie dough and the top-shelf scotch none of them had ever quite liked.

Piper twisted the matching ring—the same as Anj's except for the copper-flecked sunstone in the middle—on her own finger as she shifted her worried gaze to Esme, skipping down her friend's pale, too-thin frame to her elegant French manicure. On her left hand, Esme had that god-awful ginormous engagement diamond. On the other hand...nothing. When had she ditched the obsidian-inlaid ring Anj had made for her? Probably Lars "the ash-hole" Ashcraft had insisted that his rock be the only one marking her.

"Ugly thing doesn't even sparkle," Piper grumbled.

"Ez's ring?" Anjali huffed out a breath. "I know, right? It's gotta be almost three carats, and it sits there like a boiled puffball mushroom."

"Maybe we can get her to hock it for dollar bills and we'll go to that male revue we saw on the billboards coming into town." Piper kept her tone light, but she watched her friend closely. Anjali had always been the first to suggest any party pandemonium; she claimed she was living up to her New Orleans heritage even though she'd left when she was a child.

Anj's hazel gaze skittered away. "I think we have a spa day tomorrow."

A spa day? Piper always felt uncomfortable being fawned over by paid strangers. And Anjali's red Creole dreadlocks weren't going to get any love in a Nevada spa. "Ez can't *be* any more polished," she protested. "This is our last chance—" She bit back the rest of her warning when their friend finally joined them in the casino entry, still staring down at her purse.

"I know I had it," she muttered.

"What's up, girl?" Anjali threaded her arm through Esme's.

"I can't find my phone."

"You had it on the plane," Piper said. "You texted Lars. Like, a dozen times."

"I must've left it." Esme turned toward the limo, her waist-length silver-blond hair swinging like a veil with the urgency of her motion. "I have to go back." The pitch of her voice rose. "He hates when he can't reach me."

Piper snagged her other arm. "You don't need it right now. The whole point of a bachelorette weekend is to get you out of each other's hair for a bit, you know? Put some mystery back in your relationship."

Although it was another damned mystery to her why Esme had agreed to Lars's proposal in the first place.

So many mysteries, so little time.

When Esme dragged her stylish leather booties, Piper tugged a little harder. "It's a private charter plane. No one is going to take your phone. It'll be waiting for you when we go back."

Unless she could convince her friend to call off the wedding. And then she sort of suspected Ez would have to get an unlisted number.

A thread of unease made her shiver, or maybe it was just the late-winter breeze snaking down from the dark desert mountains beyond the last lighted street. Piper spent her days testing for the presence of just a few microns of toxic or infectious pollutants in water samples, but she knew Esme's privileged world was even more micromanaging and potentially lethal. She wasn't going to let the heartless bastards suck the very soul out of her cheerful, gentle friend.

"Ez," she wheedled. "If you need a phone, you know you can always borrow ours." In fact, she'd already decided she was going to make Ez look at the lengthy, numerous, and progressively creepier texts Lars had been sending her—stuff about how much Esme needed to rest before the wedding, how they shouldn't drink too much, all culminating last week in a demand that Piper report to him if anything went awry during their girls' night out. At which point she'd decided with finality that *no boys allowed* was going to be the rule for the weekend. "We'll be together the whole time so we can just share our minutes. Okay?"

After a moment, Esme's backward lean relented although she let out a shuddering breath. "Without my phone, I won't know what was scheduled for us."

Anjali snorted as arm in arm they passed the flickering sconces. "Since when do you keep a schedule, Miss Sleeps-'Til-Noon? Schedules are Miss Up-At-Dawn's thing."

Piper stuck out her tongue. "At least we *know* what time it is, Miss Clocks-Are-a-Construct-of-the-Patriarchy."

"Well, they are," Anjali said. She sketched one fingertip skyward, all dozen tin bangles on her wrist falling toward her elbow with a clatter. "The arc of the celestial bodies and the flow of the seasons should be enough to guide our days and nights."

"Uh huh," Piper and Esme said together. They exchanged glances with matching smirks and it was Anjali's turn to stick out her tongue.

Laughing in a way that gave Piper hope she could remind her friends of the dreams they'd forgotten, they passed another doorway of crystal stalagmites and stalactites and stepped into the casino proper.

All three gasped together this time.

Piper had read that the Keep was one of Vegas's best-kept secrets. Terribly exclusive—and, she figured, no doubt insanely expensive—the casino catered to the kind of high rollers that rolled over other high rollers. But for all the deathly seriousness of the insane stakes at play, the Keep still abided by the Vegas rule of lavish splendor. Half primitive mountain stronghold, half high-tech Fortress of Solitude, the Keep seemed like it didn't really know what it was trying to be. Although from the steady line of gleaming Rolls Royces and custom muscle cars that had all but pushed their serviceable limo out of the way, obviously the clientele knew what *they* wanted: inside and to give up all their money. Piper had said it was silly for their little bachelorette party to stay there, since none of them gambled, but Esme had said Lars set it up and would be disappointed if they didn't enjoy themselves.

Piper just *knew* she had to get her friend to break it off. Between Esme's family and Lars, the sweet, caring roommate who'd opened her awesome apartment to one scholarship student and one dropout had become a ghost of herself, drifting and withdrawn and more pale than ever. Piper wasn't going to let that go unchallenged, even though she'd always thought herself the least of the three, the younger sister tagalong, mostly invisible beside Esme's bright beauty and Anjali's dark glamour. Once upon a time, they'd saved her when she'd been young and homesick and thinking of giving up.

Now it was her turn to save them.

"It's over for me, Rave."

Rave closed his eyes against the unwavering finality in those words. It was so dark on the upper floor of the Keep that the abyss behind his shuttered lids actually seemed brighter in comparison. The acrid stink of old smoke and scorched metal filled his lungs like the urge to roar a denial.

"It's not over." Instead of shouting, he hissed out the words one at a time, each fletched like an iron-tipped arrow to find its mark. Not that he *wanted* to hurt his blood brother and liege lord, but he needed to trigger some feeling—*any* feeling—to stave off the petralys. Once the curse had sunk too deep, Bale would turn to stone.

Literally.

But for now—for too long—the turning to stone was only metaphorical. His brother had become cold and remote, but Bale wasn't lethally locked into his rocky fate.

Not quite yet.

"I just need a little more time," Rave said. "I'm getting closer to finding a cure."

"You said that a hundred years ago."

The implicit blame chilled Rave from his solid gold cufflinks to his combat boots, and he fisted his hands on the thighs of his jeans where he knelt on the hard floor. "If you'd let me see—"

"No." The single word was as blunt and unstoppable as a bullet.

Because no one used arrows anymore.

Rave opened his eyes. If he changed, he'd be able to see, even in this stygian blackness. But the threat of his presence in shifted form might force Bale over the edge.

Besides, he didn't really want to see how far his brother had fallen.

He could guess well enough, anyway, since he felt the same tendrils of stony coldness invading his bones, aching in the depths of the night.

"I'm close," he repeated. And he hoped his brother knew he meant both to a cure and to call on. If Bale would ever deign to call on anyone.

Still blind, Rave rose to his feet and strode toward the doorway he knew was behind him.

"Rave."

The whisper rasping from the darkness made his hackles prickle. Brother by blood and camaraderie Bale might be, but he was still lord of this place.

Rave turned to face the void.

"When I'm gone, you will be the oldest among the last of us."

"Yes," Rave acknowledged. Bale had found all of the remaining Nox Incendi and brought them to the Keep. The Tribe of the Burning Night had never been large, but now they were nearly extinct.

Turning to stone—first emotions, then sensation, then body going cold and still—was the curse of their tribe, and all their fathomless riches meant nothing.

Unless he could find a way to halt and reverse the petralys.

To bring fire back to the Nox Incendi.

"You must find the heart of your treasure," Bale said. For the first time, life pulsed in his words. A thrum of urgent need. The scent of burning metal wafted through the nothingness. "You must show the others the way."

Rave curled his lip in a sneer, knowing his blood brother could see him. "That's a myth."

"*We* are myths. It's too late for me, but find your

solarys—your true mate." Bale's voice hardened. "I command it."

Rave laughed aloud. "You can't command me to find love."

"Are your ears as useless as your eyes in that shape? I just did."

Rave peered through the blackness, but of course he couldn't tell if his brother was joking. No one—not even a king—could command love. Although legend had it that a solarys was fated by a fever in her own blood to find her dragon.

"I have enough troubles," he said, "without exposing myself to the mating fever."

"That is all you should be thinking of," Bale shot back. "You have buried your dragon too deep if you don't long for your solarys."

Buried his dragon? Rave bit back an annoyed curse. Hadn't they all? But what choice did they have in this world.

"I'll find a way to stop the petralys," he swore.

There'd been a time he never would have dared walk out on his liege, but if Bale wouldn't let himself be seen... Rave slapped his hand forward and hit the elevator button. The door opened instantly, letting a rectangle of light spill into the emptiness.

He ignored the hiss and the metallic clatter behind him, just as he'd ignore the other command.

He wasn't going to chase an imaginary solarys when he had to run the Keep, hide the Nox Incendi, and cure a curse.

He'd had centuries to amass his treasure, a dragon's lifeblood, but he'd run out of time for love.

CHAPTER TWO

Down in the control room in the casino's first basement, Rave checked in with the night managers. He'd long ago learned to leash the dragon when dealing with humans. Not because he wanted to, but because he *had* to if the Nox Incendi were to survive in the modern world. Which made Bale's accusation sting all the worse. The employees knew him, they trusted him, they liked him—and still he felt the way they flinched away, just a little.

His title might be general manager, but while *general* fit who he was to the clan, there was nothing of *man* in him. The humans sensed the apex predator in him, even through his very fine linen shirt, even though their kind wouldn't believe in him.

In dragons.

And Bale thought the Nox Incendi could find their true mates among these oblivious humans? Forget it. Shifters had gone into hiding precisely because humans were a scourge on the earth: small-minded, treacherous, jealous of the power and beauty of the beast...yet too craven to embrace the passions that ruled fang and wing.

The mating fever... Rave crushed the thought, turning the diamond back to coal dust in his mind.

The Keep was humming, brimming with restless

humanity. It always was. Bale had created a place to entice the most alpha among the humans. They might not know why they were drawn to the eclectic mix of stone and steel, of ancient and cutting edge, but the melding of splendor and danger captured their imaginations and kept them coming back, always with more of their treasure. Rave suspected that on some instinctive level, they sensed the threat of the lurking dragon, and like the misguided knights of old, they couldn't help but throw themselves to their doom.

Their financial doom, anyway. Today's dragon-shifters had no need to stockpile gold coins over old bone when they could amass stocks, bonds, mutual funds, securities, futures, real estate, patents, collectibles, and art.

Of course, gold coins were still very, very satisfying.

As for old bones... Well, bones were better with some meat attached.

As he strode past the bank of CCTV screens, a flash of something caught his eye. The security guard didn't react, but Rave reversed his step for another look.

In the low light of the casino, the colors in the cameras were muddy, so why had he thought he caught a glimpse of scintillating gold?

The screen showed three young women entering the Badlands bar—not unusual in the Keep. Just as the Keep enticed the rich and powerful, the rich and powerful enticed their own milieu of followers, including opportunistic young women who might get into more trouble with gluttonous human predators than with draconic ones.

But when he looked again, Rave noted that the middle female—thin and pale-haired—was clearly one of their primary upscale clientele, despite her youth and the hesitant way she turned her head to follow the antics of the other two. The second female in the flowing skirts was gesturing animatedly above her head, remarking—if he had to guess—on the faint, glowing stars embedded in the ceiling to simulate an endless dusk.

But it was the third female—a petite, curvaceous Latina—who had caught his attention.

Despite being translated to two dimensions, her hair gleamed with a rich, lively darkness. She stood with her hands on the lush rounds of her hips over a shiny skirt, staring at something.

He forced himself to follow the angle of her gaze. She was staring at the wall... No, at the sconce in front of her.

She pushed up the sleeves of her vee-neck sweater and reached out as if questioning its reality. At the same moment, his dragon stirred, stretching against the confines of his awareness.

"Don't touch, silly girl," he whispered. "It's real. It's all real."

She jumped back, flapping her fingers. Her companions huddled around her. The blonde took her hand and examined it. The one in the flouncy skirt smacked her lightly on the back of the head, making that dark hair fly.

Rave's hand tightened into a fist, as if he could soothe that singed skin, catch those flyaway strands. Clearly she was enthralled by fire.

To his shock, his cock stiffened too, as if he could feel the phantom sensations of heat and air through the remote images. To power the sconces, the Keep tapped into natural gas reservoirs far below. And below those, there were older, stranger vapors...

He growled low in his throat, hardly more than a rumble in his bones.

The security guard seated before the screens ducked his head and glanced warily over his shoulder. "Sir, did you say something?"

"Those three," Rave said. "Who are they?"

The guard spun to his tablet, scrolling quickly through the facial recognition program. "Checked in this evening. Reserved with full service by Lars Ashcraft for Esme Montenegro. Two-bedroom suite in the Delphi wing with a connecting bedroom. Additional keycards issued to Anjali Herne and Piper Ramirez." The guard eyed Rave cautiously. "Is there a problem, sir?"

"Unlikely. You all do good work." Rave didn't blow smoke—at least not where people might see him—so the guard preened a little. A human boss might've clapped the man on the back, but Rave just gave him a nod and continued on.

While humans might be able to mentally explain away their inadvertent flinch in the presence of dragonkin, any physical contact—even glancing—turned most people into a frantic, gibbering mess. In the backs of their disbelieving brains, they remembered the pierce of talons and the bone-deep burn of dragonfire.

Yet another reason Rave knew the legend of the solarys was only that—a fantasy, born of desperate Nox Incendi turning slowly to stone. No human could withstand such violent intimate contact to become a dragon's lover.

The tribe's only hope lay with him finding a cure to the stone blight.

And that wasn't getting done with him ogling young human females.

Even if his dragon had been intrigued by the glimpse of gold.

But he found himself taking the elevator to the main floor, one boot tapping out an impatient rhythm until the door opened. He should at least make sure she hadn't injured herself enough to make a fuss that would bring unwanted scrutiny down upon them—

He strode out, not *quite* at a run.

"Watch your step, cousin."

The gruff admonition made Rave bristle and swing around at the borderline challenge.

Just as quickly, he forced himself to stand down. He blinked back the lightning he knew was kindling in his eyes. There was no cause to rouse his dragon further, no reason for such a reaction.

Torch lifted his hands, his eyebrows shooting up almost as quickly, and Rave realized the quiet growl he'd swallowed earlier had come out much louder this time.

"Where's the fire?" Torch rolled forward onto the

balls of his feet, the heavy leather of his biker boots creaking with a sound like eagerness. Even his unruly shock of dirty blond hair looked ready to rumble.

"No fire," Rave said.

But there had been a flame. And *she* had put her hand to it, too curious for her own good.

Why was he still thinking about her?

To his annoyance, Torch altered course to fall into step beside him.

"You talk to Bale?"

Rave jerked his head in a brusque nod. "Nothing's changed."

"Including him?"

After a moment's hesitation, Rave admitted, "I didn't actually see him."

Torch let out a low curse. "Not good, Rave."

He wouldn't honor that with a reply. "I need another vial of your ichor."

Torch cursed louder. "You've almost bled me dry."

"Don't be an ass. Ichor rejuvenates." Or was supposed to, at least.

"Not as fast as you take it."

"You're the youngest. If I ask any of the older ones—"

"Fuck. I know, I know. Don't ask them." Torch blew out a long breath. "I'll come by the laboratory in the morning. Just...give me a night, all right? I'll make sure there's something worthy in my veins."

"No going out to fight at the Cage Club," Rave warned him. "We have enough troubles. Don't need you wrangling with rogue dragonkin."

Torch snorted. "But *that* trouble would be fun."

If only. For the first time, Rave acknowledged the desperation gnawing at the back of his determination, undermining the belief he'd held for so long that he *would* find a way. He'd seen promise in comparing Torch's younger blood with that of the older dragon-shifters. There were biochemical differences between the two; if he could identify, isolate, and compensate for those differences, he could reverse the petralys. No dragon would be forced to rely on the fantasy of finding his solarys—the heart of his treasure. But his experiments were taking too long. With all the years that had passed him, by now he could've turned lead into gold.

If even Torch was starting to lose his ichor—if the flowing fire within him was slowly cooling and congealing—what hope was there for the rest of the Nox Incendi?

In the Badlands bar, Piper clinked her glass with Esme and Anjali, wincing a little as she jostled her burnt fingers. At least the bowl of her daiquiri was nice and cold. She was such a dumb-ass to think that fire hadn't been real.

"It's been too long," she said. "To a great girls' night out. Salud."

"Cheers," Anjali agreed.

Esme said nothing. She just drank.

Piper exchanged glances with Anj over their glasses. But Anjali looked away.

Piper frowned and kicked at her under the high table. Instead of barking a wtf at her, which she always would've done, Anjali avoided the swing of the heavy Danskos and scooted her tall chair closer to Ez.

"Esme, you never sent us a picture of your dress," Anjali said.

Piper resisted the urge to roll her eyes. So much for finding an ally in her other friend. She'd just have to launch Project Wreck-A-Wedding herself.

Esme reached for her purse then paused. "No phone." She turned toward Anj. "Can I borrow yours? I should text Lars—"

Piper drummed her burnt fingers on the table to distract them. "Lars is probably having his bachelor party. That's why he was so eager to get us out of Salt Lake City."

Esme lifted her dark gaze. Compared to her pale hair, the deep bronze of her eyes had always been a little exotic, but now, in her winter-white sheath dress with her skin almost translucent, she looked sort of...scary. "Lars wouldn't do that."

"*We're* doing that," Piper reminded her. "That's what a bachelorette party is. Having some fun. Burning off that last chance at a crazy night. Checking to make sure you really are meant to be together and that there's no one else—like, really, *anyone* else you'd rather be with..." She gave Esme a long, slow, meaningful blink.

She winced again when Anj's toe connected with her

shin. Luckily, her friend was wearing those silly ballet slippers with no follow-through.

"Speaking of burning things down..." Anjali gave Piper a meaningful look. "That whole idea of 'meant to be' is just a lot of bullshit."

Piper gaped. "Your uncle's shop sells self-help tea leaves that tell people who they should marry."

Anjali cranked her jaw obstinately to one side. "That's how I know it's all bullshit."

Esme stared down at her drink. Although she'd lifted the glass to her mouth at the toast, the level of liquor was still the same. "It doesn't matter anyway."

Piper and Anjali both eyed her warily. "What doesn't matter?" Anj asked.

"Whether it's meant to be, or if there's someone else, or if it's all bullshit," Esme said flatly. "It doesn't matter."

Piper reached across the table to touch Esme's wrist, ignoring the ache in her hand. "Oh, honey. It *does* matter. That's what I'm telling you."

Ez lifted her eerie gaze. "It doesn't matter *anymore*," she clarified. "I agreed to Lars."

Agree to him. Not *love* him. Or even *want* him.

Piper wanted to shake the blond highlights right off her head, but the thready rush of the pulse in Esme's too-delicate wrist made her afraid she might break her friend into a million pieces. "But why?" She couldn't help the plaintive whine in her voice. She had a PowerPoint on the computer back in their rooms with a mindmap she'd worked up the night after Lar's last text to review everything they'd dreamed about, the three of them, who they wanted to be. But she didn't think she was going to have a chance to remind Ez of everything she'd apparently forgotten. "Don't you remember swiping right on all those social workers and elementary school teachers? Remember that cute juggler? Why Lars?"

Esme lifted her chin, and for the first time, Piper saw Ez's blue blood in the haughty tilt. The flat line of her lips held nothing of the girl who'd delayed her holiday break European ski vacation by a day to string popcorn strands for their apartment Christmas tree. "It's not something that someone like you could understand."

Piper recoiled, and even Anj looked taken aback.

If she noticed their consternation, Esme didn't seem to care. She pushed from her seat, towering like an icy queen in her high-heeled booties. "I'm tired. I'm going back to the room. Anj, you can have the second bedroom in the suite." Without glancing at Piper, she added, "You can take the other room. Good night." She stalked away.

After a moment of shocked silence, Anjali sighed. "Nice going, Pipsqueak."

Piper sank back in her chair at the angry word that had once been an affectionate nickname. "You can't believe she wants to marry that creep."

"And you think this is how you're going to stop it?"

Sinking lower, Piper admitted, "I have a PowerPoint too. There might be a flow chart."

"Lord save me from the natural science majors." Anj rubbed her temple. "Not everything fits into tidy little boxes."

"It's called the periodic table of elements," Piper said. "And yes, all the known elements of our universe *are* on there."

Anjali's brow furrowed in annoyance. "Isn't one of the tenets of good science to face the facts? You heard Ez. She agreed to his proposal."

"Then she can just say no," Piper shot back. "She can try again."

"The world doesn't always work like that."

"You changed your major five times in three semesters. You changed boyfriends more often than that."

"And had to drop out." Anjali shoved to her feet. "While all of them dropped me. Thanks for the reminder."

"Anj, wait." Piper stood.

But her friend just held out one hand to stop her. "It's late. We're all tired. We'll have brunch tomorrow and everything will be fine." To Piper, she sounded as if she was trying to convince herself. But her glance was sharp. "It'll be fine if you get ahold of that envy."

Piper stiffened. "Envy? That's not—"

"It wasn't Esme's fault that guy ditched you for her."

"He wasn't 'that guy'. He was the faculty advisor on my independent studies, trying to sleep his way through me to Ez. And I was *delighted* to ditch *him* before I got too deep with my dissertation if that's the kind of help he was. I'm trying to save Ez from the same mistake."

"Maybe some mistakes you just have to live with."

Piper sank back into her seat, staring at her friend, her heart aching more than her reddened fingertips. "Anj, what's happened to you? You're the one who told me I could be whoever I wanted to be. You made me believe it."

Anjali's upper lip twisted just a little. "Who would've guessed I'd be so good at selling tea leaves?"

This time Piper didn't stop her when she stalked after Esme.

The three drinks, nearly untouched, looked so pathetic sitting there that Piper finished them all, one right after the other, until her burnt fingertips and her broken heart were equally numb.

CHAPTER THREE

Piper stared morosely at the trio of empties in front of her, having waved off the waitress twice already. Geez, she'd fucked up big time. She'd just wanted to make things better, like they used to be. Now her two best friends hated her. And she was alone in a very expensive Vegas bar with an open tab and a bad mood. Not. Good.

Was she just jealous of Esme's fairy tale wedding to a handsome prince? Actually, Lars was rich enough to be a king. Was she jealous of Anj's lack of responsibilities when she herself was hunkered down in the important and steady but decidedly *not* glamorous career of water quality testing?

She wished the glasses in front of her would magically refill with all those calories so she wouldn't feel so woozy. No, she wished her friends were magically the way they'd been just a few years ago, when everything seemed possible. But probably her only hope was to close out the tab and go back to her empty room in this strange place she didn't want to be before she put a big dent in her savings.

A presence loomed at her shoulder, and anger flared in her like those damn turned-out-they-were-real-flames sconces. "I really don't need anything else." Then, despite her aggravation since she'd worked for tip money before and knew it was tough, she added, "Thank you, though."

"Yes, seems like you've had entirely enough," replied a deep, smooth voice.

Piper jerked up straight. That voice... It flowed through her like the scotch she and her friends had tried when Esme turned twenty-one: silky and cool at first, but turning to fire inside.

She swiveled to face the intruder, and her heart thumping an unsteady beat, driving those inner flames out along every nerve.

He was tall; despite the raised bar seat she had to tilt her head up to look at him. He didn't try to make it any easier for her either, standing just a little too close for comfort with his hand on the back of her chair, not touching but making her acutely aware of the way her lifted chin exposed her throat.

The vee neck of her sweater suddenly seemed much too low, as if the sturdy cotton knit in burnt orange was showing off too much flesh in the valley between her breasts when not half an hour ago she'd been fretting that she looked like a schoolmarm compared to her friends.

She swallowed, tasting the sweet heat of the alcohol still burning on her tongue. She was by herself in this strange place. She needed to tell him to go away. "I'll decide when I've had enough, thanks anyway."

Whoops. That sounded less like a blow-off and more like an invitation.

His lips—the lower one fuller than the top—curled.

"You don't have to say thank you until someone gives you something you've asked for." His tone deepened another degree, like when she sank her sample collector into the water, watching it descend out of sight. "Something you want."

Something you want... "I was being polite."

"This is the Keep," he said, as if it explained everything. "That's what we play for here."

She couldn't stop her sudden grin. "Playing for keeps. So that's where it got the name. I wondered."

She knew she shouldn't stare, but she'd never been approached by such a gorgeous man. No, gorgeous wasn't quite right. On some other man those sharp cheekbones and taut jaw would be gorgeous, the tousled cocoa-brown hair would be modish. On this man...

It was like the covalent bonds of carbon: in one incarnation, carbon bonds made graphite, soft and black, but one small shift in the bonds created diamond, hard and glittering and crystal clear.

Something about the gleam in his pale blue-gray eyes took him out of the realm of all the men she'd ever known into another place. A wild, dangerous place. Her pulse raced, fast and out of control as a desert brushfire.

Or maybe that was the third drink talking.

Piper found herself leaning toward the man, the side of her breast almost brushing the backs of his knuckles gripping her chair. He smelled like the wind coming down from the mountains: wintry and resinous. From this close, she felt a little dazzled by the subtle gleam of metallic threads in his tailored dress shirt that outlined the powerful body underneath. He could easily pick her up, despite her extra few pounds, and throw her over that broad shoulder, and then he'd take her away someplace where she could see what was inside those dark dyed, slightly faded jeans...

Wait, what? Since when did she let fantasies run away with reality? Sure, he *could* pick her up, but why *would* he? Chubby chemists—hey, she needed those pounds to pad her ass from the long days sitting at her microscope—kept their fantasies to themselves. And she hadn't been interested in anything long-term anyway, not when she'd been trying to establish herself in her field. She'd always been practical, not passionate.

She forced herself to blink, to break the odd bond she felt winding between them.

"What happened to your friends?"

His abrupt question snapped her out of the haze, and she angled one elbow onto the table, listing away from him. "What friends?"

He directed his gaze toward the empties. "Nobody orders a daiquiri, a martini, *and* rum. Those don't go together at all."

"They do when their night is like mine," she muttered. With a sigh, she admitted, "My friends knocked off early. I really should join them." She grasped the corner of her chair to pull herself upright, her hand nearly brushing his.

He took a half step back, but his grip didn't leave her chair, his hand so close she swore the heat of his fingers sank into her skin. "Stay," he said softly. "One more drink. But not alone this time."

She'd gotten used to being by herself. Too smart-aleck for her hardworking parents. Two years too young for her college classmates. Too focused on getting through, getting out, getting on with her life. Until she'd met Anjali and Esme in her junior year. They'd taught her how to have fun, how to embrace the pleasures life offered. But now...

"Stay," he said again. A yearning note vibrated in his voice.

She hesitated, half out of her seat. But something pulled her back. Not gravity; gravity was actually a very weak force in the universe. Some other irresistible attraction kept her there.

Him.

And her even weaker knees, apparently.

His lips curled again, a sensuous expression that made her insides twist a little in response. "Thank you," he said with just enough emphasis that she wondered if, by staying, she was giving him more than she realized.

He angled around to Esme's abandoned seat, raising his head to stare past Piper. In an instant, the server was back.

"What can I get for you, Mr. Dorado?" She smiled wide, including Piper in the same smile. "There's a South American Carmenère that just came in. Some people are saying it's a little dark, a little too smoky, but it's intriguing, for sure."

He leaned back in his chair, hooking his elbow over the back. "You angling for the sommelier opening?"

She dipped her head. "Need to be more women in the field, sir. Why not me?"

He studied her a moment, his expression cool, then nodded. "Bring it on."

"Yes sir!" The server hustled away.

Piper stared at her new tablemate. "You work here."

"You can help me decide whether to recommend her for the position."

That wasn't quite an answer, but Piper decided it was a yes, and she studied him again with a fresh, uneasy view as if she was leaning out over a deep chasm to take one of her samples. He wasn't just some high-stakes gambler. No, he was the one sitting *above* the high-stakes gamblers, taking them for all they were worth. Which was apparently *a lot*.

So what was he doing sitting with her?

At her silence, dark lashes half shuttered his unnervingly pale eyes. "Guest servicing is part of my task list."

The way he emphasized *servicing* sent a little tremor down her spine. "I'm not really a guest. My friend Esme is the one who rolls like this." Piper waved her hand vaguely at their luxe surroundings. "I'm just...staying here."

He flashed white teeth in a quick smile. "That makes you a guest and definitely puts you on my list."

She lifted her chin. "Your list. Like taste-testing a small South American wine?"

His smile deepened, bringing out a dimple in his cheek, and his eyes gleamed like pure glacier ice struck by the sun. "It's rare enough that I might need more than a taste."

Oh boy. The quiver in her core sank right between her legs. She'd been working the dating apps off and on—mostly off because who had time for that? Now the long dry spell was trying to end itself in the dampness of her panties.

She crossed her legs in her polished denim skirt as if she could strangle the sensation. She was just having a drink, not socially lubricating a one-night stand.

The server whisked back with the wine bottle and two glasses balanced high on a tray, pristine white towel draped over her arm. The cheerful smile was gone, replaced by a serious furrow as she presented the bottle. A twinge of sympathy made Piper forget her lust for a moment. More than once, she'd been the lone female in a room of skeptical men.

She scowled at her companion, peeved—unfairly perhaps, but whatever—that he was making the would-be sommelier nervous. He arched a mocking brow at her, as if he could read her mind in the same way she and Esme and Anjali used to do.

He cleared his throat and said, "Does look intriguing. Let's open her up."

If only... Piper wrapped her ankle one more turn around her other leg, clamping her thighs tight against the renewed flood of sexual awareness.

With the first glass poured and approved, the server filled both glasses equally before letting out a relieved sigh. "Enjoy."

After she bowed her way out, Piper said, "She gets the job."

"You haven't even tried the wine yet." He handed the second glass to her on a waft of earthy, fruity fumes.

"I don't know anything about fine wines anyway. But I know she'll bust her ass for you."

He studied her with a touch of the same chilly contemplation he'd given the server. "Such a fierce champion."

Piper flushed and looked down at her glass. "Doesn't everybody need one of those?" Then she darted a look at him. Someone like him—wealthy, handsome, confident—probably hadn't ever needed a champion. People would throw themselves at his leather wing-tipped feet without him even asking, much less saying thank you.

He lifted his glass. "To—"

"I'm kind of done with cheers tonight," she said. "If you don't mind. Maybe you could just tell me your name."

"Rave."

She pursed her lips. "Mr. Dorado. Golden in Spanish. Seems an appropriate name for a guy in a casino."

"My clan...my family took the name when we came here."

She perked up. "Immigrants?" She'd always been a sucker for a good American Dream story.

"More or less. And yours?"

"Proud first generation," she said.

He smiled. "I meant your name."

She ducked her head with a chuckle. "I'm Piper."

"I hear music in that name."

"Is there madness in yours, Rave?"

He narrowed his eyes at her. A weird trick of the flickering lights made it seem as if a bolt of lightning shot across his irises. "Yes."

She tamped down another surge of the inexplicable attraction. She'd never gone for dark and dangerous guys, but... She shrugged with more devil-may-care insouciance than she really felt. "If this bottle is any good, maybe I'll sing for you later."

"If not, there are hundreds more bottles where this one came from." His gaze never left hers. "We can go through them all."

He wasn't stark raving crazy, *she* was if she thought this was going anywhere but straight to her head. And to her pussy, of course.

But maybe that was enough.

She'd give Esme and Anjali a chance to bitch about her and get some sleep. Then she'd crawl back and beg their forgiveness. At the rate she was going, by tomorrow morning, she'd have a lot of sins to her name.

Rave tipped the glass to his lips, watching as Piper did the same. Despite the lush aroma of the wine—yes, it was too dark and too smoky and very, *very* intriguing—all his predatory senses were focused on the woman across from him.

He shouldn't be here, didn't even understand why

he was. He narrowed his eyes, trying to puzzle out her allure. He had never been drawn to human females. They were too breakable. Piper had a raw vulnerability to her that made her seem fragile, but on the flipside of that was a boldness that brought him to the edge of his seat, wanting to reach across the table to put his fingertip where the glass was. To brush his thumb over the pouting curve of her lower lip while cupping his palm under the soft line of her jaw, risking the sharp nip of her teeth when she defied his natural dominance. She was a champion at heart, a protector of the innocent.

His kind ate her kind for breakfast.

It was still quite a few hours until breakfast, but he was already hungry.

So he might as well start now.

Though the wine couldn't slake his thirst, he took a mouthful, letting the loud but complex flavors swirl over his tongue.

She'd be like that, if he took her. Judging from the dusky cast to her skin and the width of her cheeks—now flushed brighter than her sweater—at least some of her ancestors had come up from the slow, warm lands to the south where these ancient grapes now thrived. Her thick, black hair looped loosely around her shoulders when she tilted her head to take a second sip.

She let out a soft hum of pleasure that speared him square in the loins. He hadn't missed the scent of her arousal earlier, but he'd put the blame on the trio of cocktails she'd tossed back. Now *his* cock wanted a chance to wring that sound from her.

When was the last time he had stirred down there? The stone blight had affected him more than he realized, leaching away even the desire for desire. Until now.

The wine slipped down his throat with a finish that had more than a hint of the char marking the barrels where it aged but still bright with a tart sweetness that lingered on his breath.

Oh yes, he would drink that again.

He waited until she lowered her glass after a third mouthful then gave her an impatient look.

She licked her lips, a move that sent a surge of blood, thicker than any wine, to his groin. "I like it." She shrugged. "That's all I really know."

"That's all you need to know." He topped off her glass. "I like it too. I'll make a note to buy out the winery's stock."

"Must be nice," she muttered.

He paused. "I thought we both liked it."

"Not the wine. I meant it must be nice to just...get whatever you want."

He gave her a hard look. "It's not always that easy."

She snorted. "Says the guy who just bought out a winery."

He took a drink, still watching her over the rim. "Not everything is for sale."

She smirked, and he realized no one had ever smirked at him. Except Torch, of course. "Oh yeah," she drawled. "Tell me one thing you've wanted that you haven't been able to buy."

"My brother's life."

The moment the words left his lips—souring the pleasurable tang of the wine—he wanted to choke them back. Hell, how high was the alcohol content on that Carmenère?

As appalled as he was at his own slip, he was even more shocked when Piper reached across the table and touched his white knuckles clenched on the stem of the wine glass.

"I'm sorry," she murmured. "That was rude of me, and mean. I'm sorry for your loss."

Her hands were square and sturdy, the somewhat short fingers decorated only by clear nail polish and one ring on her right middle finger. As if the warmth of her touch had thawed something inside him, he couldn't keep his mouth shut. His greatest fear just leaked right out. "Bale isn't dead, but he's...very sick."

And she should be running away by now, screaming, sensing the beast in him through the barest connection of their fingers.

Instead, she wrapped her fingers into his with a light squeeze. Her expressive eyes wrinkled at the corners as if she felt the pain he refused to acknowledge. "That must be hard for you, watching when you can't do anything."

How could she...? "You know," he said softly, testing the unexpected connected between them. "You've gone through it too."

She nodded. "My father fought through two bouts of cancer. He was a farm worker, made his way up to crew leader in pesticide application. He kept going back to work because we needed the money. But the third time got him." Her voice cracked.

Rave couldn't stop himself from threading his fingers between hers. "Did it ever get easier, knowing what was to come?"

After a moment, she shook her head, her eyebrows peaking as if to hold back the sheen that turned her gaze to deep, dark pools. "I think it was worse. But I was glad to be there with him at least."

A cold fury swept through Rave's body, spreading out along limbs that didn't exist when he was in this shape. He didn't want to "be there" while Bale turned to stone. He wanted to stop the petralys, even if he had to ignore his liege's commands, even if he had to drain Torch to the second-to-last drop of ichor.

He knew he was holding Piper too tightly. If he'd been merely a human male, he would scare her with this intensity. And if the dragon was rising in him...

But Piper returned the ferocity of his grip though the gentleness in her dark eyes never wavered. "Some things you can't fight. I'd kind of forgotten that myself."

"I've always fought." As he said it, he heard the weariness in his own voice. When dragonkin had gone underground, out of human memory, he'd fought to keep the Nox Incendi secret. He'd fought to keep them alive. But he was failing.

Sometimes he couldn't even remember why he was fighting, his dragon all but forgotten.

"Maybe we both need to let it go," she said softly.

Her thumb skimmed across his taut knuckles, light as a butterfly skipping over clouds. "Just for a little while."

His half-hard cock understood her before his brain did and thumped up against the fly of his jeans. He let out a short, sharp breath. "Piper..."

She tugged her hand out his, and in his surprise, he let her go. "I'm sorry," she said. "I didn't mean—"

"No." He reached for her and grabbed her wrist before she could rise. "No more please and thank you and polite words. Just...fuck yeah."

Her gaze jumped up to his, and she let out a little laugh. There was the smallest gap between her front teeth, and he found himself helplessly charmed.

This must've been how virgins had slain dragons back in the day.

But Piper Ramirez wasn't going to slay him. She didn't even know what he was. They were just both tired of fighting: fighting the passage of time, fighting for the lives of others and losing. But their mystifying mutual attraction was one fight he would willingly lose.

For whatever reason, she didn't fear him. Maybe the flavor of old fire in the Carmenère had buried the natural—and entirely reasonable—fear of getting burned.

Whatever it was, this was one night he would take for himself.

And tomorrow, he'd be back in the fight.

CHAPTER FOUR

Not letting go of Piper, Rave grabbed the wine bottle in his other hand. "Come with me."

"Where?"

"Into the heart of the Keep."

A wildness filled him, almost like the moments of shifting into the dragon, when his whole being seemed to expand with light—air and fire changing every molecule of his being.

As if the same wildness drove her, Piper slid from her seat, almost falling into his arms despite the heavy clogs. He looped one arm around the nip of her waist to steady her, and the wine bottle still in his grasp bumped against the shiny denim sleeked over her luscious ass.

Such dizzying dips and curves she had, hidden by her clothes, like air currents he couldn't touch while in this upright shape. But he was touching *her*, all over. The heady perfume of her—cinnamon and sweet raw honey, as vibrant as her fiery sweater—swirled around him. He tightened his hold on her waist, drawing her closer. Their other hands were still clenched tight, as if they were about to dance.

Surely now she sensed she was caught by a monster out of myth. Surely now she would run...

Her dark gaze dropped to his mouth, and her little pink tongue darted out to moisten her lips.

Ah hell, he'd willingly lay down for the slaying if she'd first let him drink the last of the Carmenère from the small of her back.

He tilted his head and brought his mouth swooping down on hers. The perfume of the wine, earthy and heady, all but flamed between them. He wasn't going to let anyone else touch the Carmenère, no matter how many bottles he found. It would be the flavor of her, forever, only his to savor.

She was shorter than him, enough to be awkward, but she strained up on tiptoe to meet his hungry kiss, and her lips parted to take him in.

Thank all the dragon-slaying saints, she was no virgin. She knew what she wanted, and she wanted his tongue tangled around hers.

Now that he thought about it, maybe *that* was how virgins slew: by withholding their sweet, chaste kisses.

Fuck that.

He slanted his mouth hard across hers at the same time he yanked her hips flush to his upper thigh, wedging one knee between hers and stealing her aroused gasp like the treasure it was.

His, all his.

When he finally lifted his head, her lips were red and swollen, her dark eyes glowing.

"I thought you said we were going somewhere," she said.

"Temptress," he growled. "You made me forget myself."

Red lips curled. "That sounds like exactly what I

want."

He spun her away from him and strode toward the door.

"Wait." She tugged at his hand. "I didn't pay for our drinks yet."

"I got it," he said. *I got you.*

The bone-deep certainty made his pulse fly through his veins, as if his very blood wanted to pour out at her feet.

After that, her thumping clog steps were as quick as his, and a little stumbling, like his, although he'd had only one measly glass of wine. *She* made him feel awkward and strange, as if he didn't know himself anymore, as if his body had somehow changed. And he was used to changing, so what had she done to him?

They rushed through the huge atrium, dodging gamblers and groupies and gawkers.

She craned her neck to stare up at the walkways crisscrossing the upper stories and the balconies outside of the rooms that looked down into the atrium. "Is this the heart of the Keep?"

"No. This is its grasping jaws, always open for more." They rushed past the restaurants and shops and plunged into the quieter chaos of the game rooms where craps and blackjack and roulette tables were stacked high with chips.

"Is this its heart?"

"No. This is its big, hungry belly."

He hustled her past the greedy display, knowing his own greed was worse, much worse. He wasn't content with all the sparkling trinkets in the shops or the feasts at their five-star eateries or even the fortunes to be had at the tables.

His dragon had roused and it wanted her, only her, all of her.

And it would have her.

He led her through the confusing labyrinth that made the passage of time or money irrelevant in a casino and finally pushed through an unassuming door tucked in a back alcove. The door opened to blackness.

"Where...?" She caught her breath when the sconces flared to life. "Those flames are real," she said, a hint of accusation in her tone. "Someone could get burned."

"Nobody would be so curious and disbelieving as to touch it," he chided. Then he gave her a long look.

She returned his gaze under lowered brows, nibbling at her lip uncertainly, as if she wasn't sure whether to confess or accuse him of spying.

He didn't bother waiting for her to decide and just tugged her onward.

The wide stairs spiraled down, the gold veins in the black marble glittering in the restless flicker of the sconces. Piper wouldn't be able to see to the bottom with her human eyes. Even his dragon-sharpened senses strained to pick out the way ahead.

Her hand tightened in his, and he felt the flutter of her pulse. From their headlong rush? From fear?

From excitement?

At the bottom of the stairs, one last sconce pointed the way, and he pushed through the gleaming yellow gate baring the passage.

"Is that—?" She slowed and glanced back over her shoulder as they passed.

"Gold," he said.

"You know that's crazy, right?"

He thought about it for a moment. "No."

She laughed a little breathlessly and then she was at his side again.

Just as they broke out into the heart of the Keep.

Piper felt she'd been gasping in awe and struggling to catch her breath ever since she'd climbed out of that stupid limo onto the grounds of the Keep. But this...

It was a garden—half formal and stylized with geometric plantings, half wild as if no one had been taking care of it—but at the bottom of a deep well. She knew they'd gone down and down the stairs, but she hadn't realized how far. Despite the low braziers flickering with real flames and a profusion of twinkle lights in the leaves, a tiled pool reflected only darkness, and she looked up and up to see the open night sky high above.

Unlike the atrium, there were no crossing gangplanks or overlooking balconies. The walls of the garden were perfectly smooth like the impossibly seamless marble of the stairs, though a few optimistic vines were creeping up the sides, softening the stone. Her head spun as if she were looking *down* at a long fall instead of up.

She swayed.

Rave steadied her again. "This is the heart," he said softly.

"It's beautiful." In the circle of his arms, she felt safe enough to look up and spin slowly. It was almost as if she was flying up into the night...

Rave stopped her when she was standing with her back to him. He pulled her against the broad expanse of his chest, his arms crossed in front of her. "You're beautiful," he murmured into her hair.

She leaned back into his strength. "Everything here is beautiful. You've made a dream world. I didn't think I'd fall for it, but I guess I did."

"I'll catch you." His words, scarcely louder than his breath, teased her ear, and she shivered.

His arms tightened possessively. "Are you cold?"

She shook her head. "Even though I can see the stars."

"Geothermal heat and angled mirrors keep everything alive." A note of diffidence crept into his voice. "Even things that shouldn't be here."

She plucked the wine bottle from his lax grasp and took a long swallow. Yet another gasp as the reckless rush of wine swirled through her.

She turned within the confines of his embrace and held the bottle to his mouth. "Maybe these things *shouldn't* be here, but they *want* to be here," she said. "Drink."

His pale blue-gray eyes half shuttered, he let her tip the wine and drank deep. But the angle was awkward and when she pulled back, a droplet of wine stained his lower lip, gleaming in the firelight.

She surfed up his chest to lick the blood-red bead from the soft flesh. When she lowered herself, other parts of him were *not* so soft.

She stared up at him wonderingly, feeling a little cross-eyed. "This is a secret place, isn't it?" The cathedral silence, unbroken except for the muted splash of water, made her whisper the question.

"Yes."

"Why are you showing me?"

"Because you came." He scowled as if that answer didn't satisfy him any more than it did her. "Because you let me take you."

"Oh." *Yes, take me.* She wanted to say it aloud, but apparently there were limits to how far even a bottle of wine on top of three cocktails could take her. She gazed up at him, forcing her eyes to focus on his, hoping he would see what she couldn't say.

Gently, he pried the bottle from her hand and set it aside on the tiled rim of the pool. For a heart-stopping moment, she thought he was going to do the same to her. But then he put one finger under her chin and tipped her head up. Above him, the night sky was a perfect circle of blackness and stars, and nearby, something was blooming with the wild fragrance of a hothouse flower that didn't care about seasons and demanded to be indulged and admired.

Indulged like Esme, admired like Anjali. Meanwhile, Piper had always been the weedy daisy, struggling to grow on the side of the road. But for once, she was in the beautiful, secret place with the gorgeous, mysterious man.

This sort of thing never happened in her organic chem and statistics books. This was a fantasy romance, pure and simple as water.

Rave brought his mouth down on hers as gently as the warmth steaming up from beneath their feet. When he deepened the kiss, the heat between them rose, as if they were falling to the center of the roiling, molten earth.

She clung to him, her fingers wrapped tight around his biceps. Through the thin linen of his expensive dress shirt, she felt his muscles tighten, as if it was everything he could do not to grab her.

She wanted to be taken. The wanting burned in her like a fever, spiraling ever higher.

She transferred her grip to the front of his shirt. The buttons were tiny, so tiny, and her eager—okay, and drunken—fingers only got the first one undone before she lost all patience. She gripped both sides and wrenched the fabric apart, sending those tiny buttons popping.

"Piper..."

Was that a gasp from him this time? At least she wasn't alone in that. "Yes," she breathed out the word. "Oh yes."

She ran her hands down the skin she'd exposed. Under her wandering fingertips, his pecs bunched and the washboard muscles of his abdomen clenched.

He let out a long, anguished hiss, and she glanced up uncertainly.

"Rave..."

"Don't stop. Don't ever stop."

She pushed the linen back from his shoulders, and the writhing muscles were even harder there. Good heavens, did he carry all the wine from South America himself?

She leaned forward to brush a kiss along the flexed musculature of his chest. And with his flushed, heated skin just a few inches from her nose, she noticed...

"You're shining."

He cupped the back of her head. "You're killing me. Don't stop."

"What? No, I'm serious. What are these?"

"Nothing. Tattoos. They're nothing."

She stripped the shirt entirely off him. The fine linen drifted silently to the stamped tile beneath their feet. Tracing her fingers over him again, this time more slowly, wonderingly, she followed the lines of all the tattoos.

"Wow," she breathed, struggling to focus her vision. Flowers, moons, a mountain range, a butterfly?, something with rather scary fangs, a bunch of chemical symbols she knew from her own work and other symbols that seemed familiar and yet not. Despite her effort to concentrate, her vision seemed to whirl even more, blurring the lines in a way that made them come weirdly alive. In the twinkle lights, the ink seemed to fade then brighten as he moved restlessly under her hands. "So many. So different."

"So not why I brought you here."

She wrinkled her nose at his rudeness. "Why? Are these supposed to be secret too?"

After a moment, he jerked his head in a brusque nod. "Most people...don't notice them."

"I suppose not with your shirt on." She gave him a wry grin.

Another long moment, then the harsh set of his lips softened. "Oh yeah. Forgot about that."

"Is it, like, blacklight ink?"

"Sort of. But really, it's—"

"Nothing. Yeah, I heard you. But they are beautiful too." She circled the one place on his chest that wasn't marked, just above his heart. "Missed a spot."

"I'm...waiting on that one."

Something in his tone made her finger curl away as if she'd almost burned herself. Again. But she knew all about keeping some places untouched.

So she traced down his midline. Each muscle rippled behind her stroke, and his breath roughened. When she arrived at the button of his jeans, she paused. "I don't think I can rip this one," she said sadly.

He huffed, not quite a laugh. "You could ask for my help."

"Nah. I'll muddle through somehow. I got this."

"You do," he said softly.

She looked up at him through her lashes, wondering what was going on inside him. Well, not inside his jeans; she could figure that out well enough.

Why had he chosen her? Why had he brought her here when any old room would have been fine by her?

Very carefully, she undid the button of his fly and eased down the zipper. Each tick of the zipper teeth made his breath hitch. Her own muscles ached with the urge to hurry, before this odd, sensual encounter ended like a dream. But she refused to squander the chance, lingering over each millimeter of revelation, inhaling the spicy fragrance of his warming skin.

"Commando?" she murmured. "You must trust me."

"Trust you? You know you're torturing me, right?" His voice was strained and his hands were fists at his side.

She leered up at him and slid her fingers past the zipper. "I'm sort of getting the impression you like it."

"I want you to know *you* can trust *me*," he said hoarsely. "You've seen all of me." He hesitated. "All of me that matters."

"Not quite all..." She pushed at his waistband.

With a quickness, he kicked out of his jeans, wing-tips and socks going too. Then he stood before her gloriously naked.

She let out a long, slow breath. Never mind the one-armed bandits upstairs, she'd hit the jackpot down here. How had she gotten so damn lucky?

The width of his heavy shoulders narrowed to lean hips and a triangular thatch of dark hair that framed the thick shaft of his erection thrusting upright to his navel. The soft foliage of the garden behind him and the exotic tilework only made his utter maleness more enticing.

Piper licked her lips in anticipation and blushed when his cock swelled up another degree.

"Oh," she said faintly. "*Por el amor de Dios...*"

"You're not going to run off now, are you?" When he put his fists on his hips, the blunt head of his penis waggled in disapproval.

"Not hardly," she said.

"Very hard," he countered.

She giggled. Maybe a little hysterically. She put her fingers over her lips and stared at him.

"Come here." He crooked his finger at her and she felt it like he'd touched her mouth. No, she felt it like he'd roped her whole body and soul and was slowly reeling her in. "I want to see you too."

Step by step, she closed the distance between them. The heat of his bare skin all but scorched her, right through her clothes. If she was naked too...

She looked up at the stars far above. "Can anyone else see?"

He reached out and wrapped his hand gently around her throat. "Do you want others to see us?"

She gave a little shake of her head, as much as she could against the confines of his grasp. "No. No one else."

"That's good," he murmured. "Very good. Because I should warn you: I don't share. What's mine is mine."

An irresistible shudder wracked her, and she felt as if only his touch was holding her upright.

He tilted his head. "You're shy."

"No. I..." She swallowed against his palm. "I'm just

not good at this."

He stroked his hand up the column of her throat to brush his knuckles over her cheek. "You are perfect at this."

A strange heat followed his touch, and she leaned into him. "It was the wine." Which had worn off long ago, she realized, burned away like morning fog. "Where's the rest of it?"

He tsked. "I don't want to fuck the empty bottle. I want to light you up." His glittering gaze raked her. "But where to start..."

She swayed, lightheaded not with booze but with lust. "Rave," she whispered. "I need you to touch me. All over. Make me burn."

With a strangled curse in some language she didn't know, he stripped her bare, skirt and sweater banished, Danskos landing somewhere behind her with a clunk. His hands were everywhere, and still she wanted more. Sparks and lightning and full-on bonfires bloomed everywhere he touched, and her cleft was drenched with dampness, as if trying to put out the flames. But she wanted the fire as she'd never wanted anything before, with a pure and simple desire for pleasure.

He was teasing her, she knew, though his jaw was tight with the effort of holding himself back. When he was done, he stood back, eyeing her. Her skin prickled everywhere his gaze passed, each tiny hair rising and falling in a wave as if at his wordless command. But she didn't feel exposed, she felt freed, like Eve wandering the garden before the Fall. And she already knew where the snake was...

"Where's the rubber tree?"

Rave grunted. "Hold on." He twisted around to reach for his jeans. He'd draped their clothes over the ledge that framed the pool. He withdrew the foil square. "I feel I must explain. I saw you on the security cameras. That is why I went to find this before I found you."

Okay, that made her feel a little exposed. But she put one hand on her canted hip, letting him get an eyeful of what the cameras *hadn't* seen. "I guess the house really does always win."

"I'll make sure you get your fair share." He sat back on the ledge, his thighs spread. "Come to me."

She hastened toward him and he took her hand, guiding her to kneel astride his lap, facing him. The tile under her knees was unforgivingly hard but smooth as flower petals. That minor discomfort was forgotten as Rave's big hand cupped her mound.

"You're so wet for me already." He pressed against her labia, teasing the hidden nerves around her clit, and she shivered with the fever of wanting him.

"It's been awhile," she admitted.

"Longer for me, I'm guessing."

Was that why he'd chosen her? Even as the self-consciousness reared in her, she battered it down. He could've had any woman in the Keep, probably.

But he'd seen *her*. He'd come for her.

For once, she'd be the greedy one, and she'd treasure this moment forever.

CHAPTER FIVE

Rave held back a mighty groan when Piper braced her hands on his shoulders and writhed slowly against his palm, working herself in a circle until the base of his thumb grazed the swollen nub of her clit. Damp, slick heat coated his fingers as he tested her readiness.

She moaned and impaled herself on his hand, grinding down hard.

Oh fuck yeah, she was ready.

Still palming her, he smoothed the condom down his aching cock. *Do. Not. Come. In own hand.* But her needy little whines were driving him mad.

Sure, that was his excuse now. But what in the name of the skies had made him bring her to his secret place?

This was his lair, where he shifted and flew, out of sight, where he kept his treasure hidden.

So many secrets. No wonder he'd felt compelled to strip himself bare in front of her, even if he couldn't tell her a thing.

But she hadn't fled from his touch. She welcomed it, sought more of it, if her heaving pants were any indication. And the clench of her knees around his hips held him fast. He tried to keep himself a little apart, but her pleasure spread through him like a fever.

In a haze, he centered his cock at her slick opening and with exquisitely agonizing slowness, speared her to the core.

She tilted her head back, her dark eyes closing in ecstasy. Her fingers spasmed on his shoulders, driving muscle down to bone. She was stronger than she looked.

He thrust up into her depths, gritting his teeth against the urge to launch her into the air with the force of his poundings. Her every little mewl, each little grind, whittled away at his control.

Good thing he had centuries of stone built up around him, or she would have wrecked him with one whimper.

But his stone couldn't last against the relentless onslaught of her wet heat. She would crack him apart...

He fisted his hand in her thick, black hair, cranking her head back farther. She thrust her breasts out, the heavy globes coming right into reach of his teeth. Lush with the sugar-and-spice scent of her arousal, her dark gold skin gleamed in the firelight, richer than anything in his ancient hoard.

He swirled his tongue along one dusky areola, bringing the flesh to a peak as hard and blood-red as a raw, uncut ruby. He had more than a few of those. Next time, he would pour the gems around her and watch her eyes gleam with awe.

Next time...

The shock of his own wayward thoughts made his jaw clench, and he bit down harder than he meant to. She bucked against him with a sharp cry, a fresh gush of heat clamping on his cock.

Oh, so she liked a touch of roughness.

He kissed her bitten breast, lashing the hurt with the softness of his tongue until she moaned.

Then he bit her again.

She screamed and orgasmed with a power that nearly knocked them into the pool. Only the strength of his legs braced against the tile kept them from going over backward.

He forced her hips flush with his, riding each spasm of her pussy like the stormy gusts that would either crush him to the earth...or fling him to the sky.

Letting her come halfway down, he stroked one hand across the small of her back, tracing the unseen dimples framing her spine. That was where he'd pour the Carmenère. When her breathing had almost steadied, he brought his hand around between them, flicked her clit and sent her off again like a bottle rocket.

And this time he followed.

He pumped his hips up into her, bouncing her, until with a hoarse shout he came.

His muscles locked with the force of his ejaculation, lifting her higher. She clung to his shoulders, her fingers driving muscle to bone, hard enough to leave a bruise if he'd been a man. Definitely stronger than she looked.

As his ass settled back to the ledge—more shaky than that time he was struck by lightning while flying through a desert thunderstorm—she tucked her head into the crook of his neck.

He wished that somewhere among his treasures he had something soft, a bed maybe, or at least a blanket. But he'd never needed either one before.

"Piper," he murmured.

"Shh." Her breath tickled his neck. "Don't ruin the magic with man-speak."

He opened his mouth to scoff that man-speak wouldn't happen with him considering he was a— What the hell? Had he almost told her he was a dragon-shifter?

He choked down the words. Some secrets were not his to share. "I was just going to say hold on while I get you off your knees. They must ache."

"I'll never walk again," she agreed solemnly. She lifted her head to look down at him. "Because from now on I'll fly."

She smiled, flashing the gap between her teeth, and though he'd thought every muscle in his body was entirely sated, something in his chest constricted.

The confession beat in his throat, struggling to emerge. "That good, huh?"

She nodded. "Thank you."

"Back to being polite?"

She tilted her head, dark hair looping over her shoulders to brush his pecs with an airy kiss. "I could say fuck you, but it would kind of mean the same thing."

He tightened his grip and rose to his feet, with her still riding his cock. She squeaked and wrapped her arms and legs entirely around him.

It felt...

Good.

He didn't want to put her down.

But he always felt that way about treasures he found.

Even if not all treasures were his to keep.

He strode with her to the other side of the pool where a waterfall just a little taller than him plunged over the tile. Reluctantly, he lifted her off his cock and let her slide down his chest.

As soon as she stepped away, his body began to chill. And he was a dragon—he always ran hot.

Discreetly, he disposed of the condom. In days of yore, all a dragon's pieces and parts had been considered priceless. Once upon a time, she might've bought half a kingdom with his cum.

Not that he could tell her so.

She winced a little, but her gaze was on the waterfall. "It's all like a dream..."

"I'm real." As he peeled off the condom, the words emerged from him with more force than he'd intended. It didn't matter what he said; if he tried to explain what he was, she wouldn't believe him, no matter what words he used.

Not that he wanted to tell her. He couldn't. The Keep was the last stronghold for the Nox Incendi. He wouldn't risk their existence—precarious as it was—on the passing infatuation of one young human female.

As delectable as she was.

She slanted a sidelong glance at him. "Oh, I know *you're* real. I'll have bruises to show for it."

He drew a breath to apologize—hell, now he was becoming polite because of her; next he'd be asking forgiveness for the treasures he took—but the satisfied purr in her voice told him she didn't mind. With a growl, he crowded her toward the waterfall.

"Well, if everything else is a dream, there's no point waking up now," he said. "It's after midnight."

She skipped back from him a step, grinning. "Midnight? Uh oh, are you going to turn into a pumpkin on me? I should run away before you ruin the fantasy for me."

"I'm not a fan of fairy tales." He stalked her to the edge of the pool.

"Why not? You're obviously the handsome prince."

"No," he growled. "I'm the beast."

She laughed. "Same, same."

Then she squealed as he grabbed her again and lifted her into the pool. She lifted her knees, trying to keep her feet out of the water, and nearly kicked him in the balls.

"No, no, it's going to be cold," she yelped. "Don't you dare drop me!"

He never would.

But he backed her into the waterfall. She clutched at him, stiffening. Until the first droplets hit her.

"It's warm," she said wonderingly.

He gave her a smug smile. "Geothermals, remember?"

"Oooh." She leaned back in his embrace to let the water sheet across her. Despite the heat, her nipples pebbled in sensual delight. He couldn't stop himself from dipping his head to lick at the aroused flesh, tasting the faint mineral tang of the water and the musk of her sated desire.

She sighed and squirmed, her slick pussy dangerously close to his swelling cock. If he sheathed himself inside her, skin to skin... Reluctantly, he eased her to her feet and let her frolic in the waterfall.

"This is amazing," she cried. "I could live like this forever." She spun in a circle, flinging a rainbow arc of spray through the sprinkle lights toward him.

The droplets spattered his skin sharper than acid, her cheerful declaration biting deep.

She must've felt his sudden stillness or maybe caught a glimpse of his expression, which he knew he hadn't controlled fast enough. Because she looked stricken, her dark eyes going wide. She backed into the waterfall as if the clear flow could hide her.

"I mean, not literally, obviously," she stuttered. "Just for tonight. Er, just for the moment."

He'd ruined her innocent joy. Maybe she wasn't a virgin in the classical meaning of the word, but she was so...pure. And he'd marred that, even though he hadn't shown her his fangs or talons.

Maybe that was for the best. There could be nothing between them anyway—dragon and girl.

Despite its name, in the end, the Keep never truly kept anything.

Piper wanted to curl up into a little ball and die. Stay here forever? What a faux pas of one-night stand etiquette!

Judging from the frozen set of Rave's jaw, he was

trying to figure out how to 86 her without too much embarrassment.

But here she was naked and wet under his waterfall.

And that wasn't even a euphemism.

She stepped out of the spray and squeegeed her hands down her body. When his piercing gaze followed the gesture, some devilish part of her couldn't help but slow down, easing over each curve. Of which she had many, so it took awhile.

And he watched the whoooole time.

Maybe he wanted to kick her out, but she was going to make sure he knew what he was missing. Every little bit of her.

"Uh, I don't suppose you have a towel in this garden of paradise?"

His eyes snapped up and his brow furrowed as if he didn't understand what she was saying. Then wordlessly he turned to a cabinet hidden by the vines and presented her with a long, silky robe, black and masculine.

"Will this do?"

She accepted it with a nod, though the material—oh wow, real silk—wasn't exactly absorbent. From her quick glimpse into the cabinet, there weren't any other towels or robes.

This *wasn't* a place he shared with anyone else.

As she wrapped herself almost twice in the silk, she breathed the scent, not musty exactly, but mossy, as if it didn't get used much. How did he dry himself? Did he just lounge nude in the tropical warmth until the beads of water evaporated?

She licked her lips. How she'd like to see that...

Or maybe he just didn't come here much, as lovely and fantastical as it was. Which seemed like a waste and unbearably sad at that. But he was obviously done with her, and really, she'd had enough today of people being done with her.

"Piper," he said.

She whisked over to him and touched his lips, stopping whatever he might say next because the only thing worse than him turning into a pumpkin would be him turning into a jerk. "This was all a dream," she said. "Thank you."

When he opened his mouth as if he was still intent on saying something, she pinched his lips together, sort of gently but not too gently.

"Stay right here." She let him go and stepped back, letting the robe fall from her shoulders. She thrust the damp, body-warmed silk at him. "I want to remember you just like this."

She turned to her discarded clothes and quickly dressed. The vee neck snagged on her humid skin and the polished denim didn't want to go up over her booty, as if trying to hold her back. Too bad. Twisting her wet hair into a hard, tight bun, she tried to ignore the droplets snaking down her spine, making her shiver. She hopped on one foot then the other, tugging on her Danskos over her damp feet.

When he took a step toward her, she held out her hand and straightened. "Stay," she said resolutely. "I can find my own way back." She spun on her heel, then cast one glance over her shoulder. "But I'm going to take the last of the wine."

The stunned expression on his face—his blue-gray eyes a little wide, his jaw a little slack—was worth the twinge of regret at leaving him. But she'd have to leave eventually anyway, so better to do it on her terms.

She snagged the Carmenère—boo-hoo, there was hardly any left, not enough to black out the rest of the night—gave him a little goodbye waggle of her fingers and sashayed said booty toward the golden gate.

Should she look back again or not?

Not, she decided. For the sake of her pride if nothing else.

A strange sound behind her, metallic, like the falling of coins, followed by a low roaring-rumble like distant thunder, almost made her turn. But nope, she was getting out while the glow was still good.

If she slammed the gate a little harder than was really appropriate considering the thing was probably worth millions of dollars, well, probably all poor fairy tale girls had a temper, just nobody ever mentioned it.

The black marble stairs were more of a pain in the ass going up than going down, and she wished she'd asked about an elevator. Sheesh, did he make this climb all the time? No wonder he was such a hard body. Wait, not going to think about his body too much, or she'd just be bummed she left him back there. Because that had been the best orgasm of her life, such fire and force exploding through her and leaving every nerve shimmering like a shattered diamond.

She paused next to one of the stupidly dangerous sconces to catch her breath and took a swig of the wine.

"Once burned," she grumbled at the flame.

Did it flare a little higher at her complaint? Weird. Probably just because she'd breathed on it.

She marched on.

At the top of the stairs, she peeked out through the door. Rave had said it was his secret place, and she wanted to honor that.

But she didn't see anyone around so she whisked out and—

"This hall is out of bounds for guests," growled a voice behind her.

With a muffled shriek, she bounded upright, her hand over her pounding heart. Where had *he* come from?

The man was as big as Rave but dressed like an enforcer in black leather instead of Rave's sleek linen. The short sleeves of his black t-shirt revealed full-sleeve tattoos. Not black ink, or even bright colors, but strangely metallic so that they flashed visible only when he turned a certain way into the light. Like Rave's.

Were all the men of the Keep required to have sexy, mysterious markings like this? Were they gang members of an underground mafia? And she'd given herself to one of them?

Whatever, it wasn't like she was going to see him again.

"I was just leaving." She squelched the automatic

sorry that tried to squeak out. Maybe Rave had broken her of her knee-jerk politeness. That was really just fear that she didn't belong.

Well, technically she *didn't* belong here.

And the scowl on the enforcer's face made that very clear. "Don't move."

She edged around him. "I was just going back to my room—"

"Do. Not. Move." His eyes gleamed ferociously.

She swallowed as her knees locked in place, like her Danskos were glued to the floor.

His glare pinned on her, he tapped something into his phone. One quick glance at whatever came back, an irate grunt, and then he stepped back. "You can go."

She lifted her chin and marched past him.

"Stay in the lighted areas. There are things behind the curtain you don't need to see."

She refused to answer that.

It was too late anyway.

She felt his gaze boring into her back as she hustled down the hallway. The maze of the casino that had seemed like such an adventure when Rave was holding her hand now seemed interminable and frustratingly confusing. To her dismay, her eyes prickled with tired tears when she finally found the elevator to the Delphi wing where their rooms were.

She remembered from her chemistry classes that the Greek oracle at Delphi may have taken "divine" inspiration from hallucinogenic gases rising from the spring waters. Maybe there were party drugs in the geothermal springs under the Keep. That would explain why she...

No, she wasn't going to make excuses. Esme and Anjali might have excuses for why they were giving up their dreams, but—wine aside—she'd known exactly what she was doing. And exactly who she was doing it with.

She swiped the back of her hand across her eyes— she was *not* going to be one of those girls who cried after awesome sex—wishing she could just pack up and leave. But first she had to make things right with Ez and Anj.

Tomorrow, though. As she made her way down the quiet hall, the chaos of the casino felt a million miles away. And considering how far she'd walked, it practically *was* a million miles away. The room door yielded to her key, and it was elegant as hell but there was no lush waterfall or sexy, powerful man...

She glugged down the last of the wine. There, that was done. And everything would be all right tomorrow.

CHAPTER SIX

Everything was fucked.

Rave stared at the flasks in front of him, partly filled with dragon ichor, but all he saw was the half-empty wine bottle swinging jauntily in Piper's fist. His fingers rested on the knife he'd used to take his latest sample—the blade was cast from the iron ore of a meteorite and the hilt from polished bone—but all he felt was the silk of her skin, finer than the rare weave of his robe. His cock knocked at the back of his fly, thinking it was time to come out and play, but he was stuck in his laboratory in the lowest bowels of the Keep, waiting for—

"What the hell were you thinking?" Torch slammed through the lab door.

Rave kept staring at his experiments for a long minute, waiting for his erection to sullenly subside.

Only then did he swivel on the high backless stool to face his cousin. "I was thinking you weren't going to show, so I took a sample of my own ichor. You can just leave." He swiveled back to stare blindly at his pointless, hopeless task.

Torch stomped up beside him, his blunt features warped in a scowl. "You shouldn't stick yourself when you can't afford to lose any more ichor. You know you're almost as bad off as Bale."

"Not quite yet." But almost. When he'd told Piper it

had been awhile for him, he hadn't actually done the math. But he had this morning, and it was...a long time. How had he not realized how long it had been since he took pleasure in anything?

He'd been so focused first on amassing his treasure and then trying to find a way around the stone blight that he hadn't realized how far the cold stillness had crept over him.

Hadn't noticed until Piper left and it came slithering back.

The agony had sent him to his knees with a choked cry. The dragon had swept over him, spreading its wings against the threat it couldn't see. But that only made the petralys worse. To protect him and its treasure, the dragon would take over completely, and then his fate— like a tomb—would be sealed.

If Bale felt it worse... Rave couldn't imagine the torment.

"Well, I'm here now," Torch said. "You might as well stick me."

Helpless fury twisted in Rave's belly. "I told you to go. It's too late. It's done."

Torch slammed his palm down on the table, making the flasks jump. "I was late because I was watching to make sure your conquest from last night stayed in her room and didn't go sneaking back to take a memento or two."

Without conscious thought, Rave was off the stool, on his feet, and in Torch's face. He was a fraction taller but Torch had a few kilos on him.

The fight would be fucking epic.

Behind him, the ichor flasks chimed delicately though nothing was touching them, and Rave and Torch were utterly still. The scent of scorched metal swirled in the closed room.

"Stay away from her," Rave whispered. "Don't touch her. Don't look at her. Just...don't."

After a long moment, Torch put up his hands and took a step back. "I didn't know."

Rave let out a slow, hissing breath. "You never know shit." But then he couldn't stop himself from asking, "Didn't know what?"

"That she is your solarys."

Rave flinched back, gripping the table to steady himself. The crystal flasks clanked a warning. "She... What? No. Piper isn't my true mate. She's just a human female passing through."

Torch crossed his massive arms over his chest and shrugged. "I dunno. You've never freaked out about a female before. You've never let one into your garden. Shit, I've wondered sometimes if you'd forgotten you were a beast." He stared hard at Rave. "Did you let her see you shift?"

"No!" But if she'd turned around before passing through the golden gate... "Of course not," Rave said in a more measured tone. "As I said, she's a human. She can never know."

"But if she's your true mate—"

"She's not. That's impossible. The Nox Incendi solarys are extinct." As the Nox Incendi dragons would soon be if he couldn't reverse the petralys.

But Torch had on his obstinate face. "Why can't she be your mate?"

"She is human," Rave said with exacting slowness, as if to an idiot. Which he sometimes thought Torch liked to play, if only to cause trouble. "The solarys were...special. But that was a long time ago."

"This Ramirez chick is special too," Torch said, speaking almost as slowly as Rave had. "Special to you."

"No she's not."

"Oh. My mistake. Then I guess I'll go fuck her—"

With a roar, Rave charged his cousin and drove him across the room with a forearm braced across his throat. Letting no more of those foul words pass his lips. Rave would kill him first.

But Torch didn't fight back, just eyed him with one brow cocked. "See?" he croaked. "Special."

Rave realized the iron knife was in his other hand and he jerked back with a curse. "Idiot."

Torch smirked at him. "Which makes you what? Because I still saw it before you did."

"There's nothing to see." Rave shoved him, but his cousin was too mountain-like to be moved by a mere punch. "Because she isn't my mate. Now get out of here before your ridiculousness infects my samples."

He stalked back to his experiments.

The alchemists of old had listed many uses for dragon blood, dragon teeth, dragon scales, dragon breath. They had endless recipes and incantations, each more implausible than the last. Few of them had ever seen much less killed a dragon. But it was Nox Incendi ichor where the real magic happened.

And the death.

Only the purest crystal flasks could contain ichor which had all the most dangerous properties of molten lava, corrosive venom, and toxic gas. But ichor could also heal, induce visions, transform the elements—lead into gold, anyone?—plus much more.

Right now, though, he was using it merely as a barometer of how much longer Bale could survive.

The largest flask had only a few drops within. But the substance that should've looked like translucent, opalescent quicksilver, moving restlessly of its own accord and shooting off the occasional incendiary spark, instead resembled a motionless chip of half-melted tar, dull and cold.

When it froze entirely...

But he wasn't going to let that happen.

He'd tried various methods of invigorating the ichor: adding reactive chemicals, setting it on fire, chanting spells at it, *swearing* at it. He'd tried that last one a lot. Without positive results. Hell, without *any* results.

When he'd come to the laboratory this morning, he'd wondered why he'd never lost hope.

Then he realized he'd stopped feeling hope. Stopped feeling anything at all. He was just going through the motions.

Eventually, even the motion would stop. And then he'd be like his liege, trapped in the dark, frozen, doomed.

Torch was a bastard as well as an idiot to try to give him back that hope.

In a vicious twist of retaliation to show Torch how wrong he was, Rave reached for the flask that contained his own ichor that he'd drawn earlier. He'd set it aside, waiting for it to settle into its quiescent state before he started another round of tests, but where had he put it?

The only unlabeled flask on his bench was one from a much younger dragon, less stone-bound even than Torch...

Rave stared at the flask then slowly drew it toward him. The quicksilver shimmered with miniature bolts of lightning at the disturbance, barely settling when he centered it in front of him.

The flask opening was fitted with a crystal stopper aligned perfectly to the hole so nothing could escape. This morning, he'd noted that though the containment was properly sealed, the stopper had an almost imperceptible crack in the crystal. Nothing to cause a problem, but the tiny flaw had caught the light with a cheery sparkle and made him think—for no good reason—of the imperfect gap in Piper's smile. How he'd wanted to see it again...

This was *his* ichor.

Which was impossible.

With a shocked oath, he scrambled for the huge, leather-bound journal where he'd kept notes going back before the advent of computers. He'd known he might have to pass his work to another if the stone blight overtook him first.

He flipped quickly through the pages. When was the last time he'd taken his own ichor?

There. He slammed his finger on the entry, as if he could pin the memory down exactly.

New bakery in the Keep. Can't remember the scent of cinnamon but staff says it smells divine. Collected another deep draw. Ichor is darkening. Ash colored with oily streaks. Sluggish and non-conductive except with most highly reactive compounds. Sample destroyed in alchemical trial #147.

Rave didn't bother consulting the outcome of trial #147. It had been a failure, whatever it was. All the trials had been failures.

But now... This ichor—*his* ichor—was throwing off the corruption of the petralys.

"How?" he whispered.

"The solarys," Torch said. "I told you."

Rave twisted around. He'd forgotten his cousin was even there. "Humans can't touch the ichor. They don't have any magic."

Torch spun slowly on the stool he'd claimed. "Witches and warlocks have magic," he pointed out as he came around again.

Rave frowned. "Humans don't believe in magic any more than they believe in dragons. Those days are gone."

"We're still here." Torch spread his big hands. "Even if we're in hiding. Maybe they're in hiding too."

Bolting off his seat to get away from the changed ichor, Rave scraped one hand down his chin as he paced.

"Piper is not a witch."

Torch pursed his lips. "You're probably right about that," he agreed reluctantly. "As far as I can tell, Piper Ramirez is exactly what she seems to be: daughter of a migrant farm worker, first kid to college on financial and merit scholarships, made good, paid to bring over some close family members. Seems like the weirdest thing she's ever done is become friends with a rich bitch and a hippie love child." He peered at Rave. "Now aren't you glad I looked her over for you?"

Rave snarled at him soundlessly. "If she's not an alchemist—"

"Well, she *is* a chemist. Works with a company doing water quality control." Torch grinned a little goofily. "She makes water pure. Isn't that sweet?"

Rave took a threatening step toward his cousin before he could force his boots to a halt. He spun back to the ichor, swirling with faint rainbows like the surface of a bubble. "If she's *not* an alchemist," he said firmly, "if she doesn't have magic, how can she be influencing the ichor?"

"It's not what she is, exactly," Torch said. "It's what she is to *you*: your solarys."

Something inside Rave thundered, a wordless cry he couldn't interpret. A warning from his dragon? "I admit something is reversing the effects of stone blight on the ichor," he said. "But why her? Why now?"

Torch shrugged. "Does it matter? You found her."

If she was a solarys. Maybe part of him had become too human, because he couldn't make himself believe.

"I'm not going to give her to Bale until I know how and why this is happening."

Even as he said the words, the roar within him turned deafening. But he didn't need his ears to see Torch's jaw swing open in surprise.

Over the cacophony in his own head, Rave said, "Our liege must be saved if the tribe is to survive." That the Nox Incendi existed still was only because Bale had driven himself remorselessly on their behalf. Bale Dorado was their liege, but more than that, he was their guiding light. The survival of the Nox Incendi depended on their liege being alive and strong enough to hold their dragons in check. Without him, the tribe would literally fly apart.

The chaos inside Rave froze at that truth, and the shivering rainbows in the ichor burst.

"You can't deny your true mate," Torch said softly. "You'll turn to stone."

"But the Nox Incendi will go on."

Even if he had to sacrifice Piper Ramirez.

CHAPTER SEVEN

Piper woke late with sticky eyes and the taste of old wine in the back of her throat.

Ugh. She stumbled to the luxurious bathroom that, nice as it was, didn't have a waterfall.

Or a lover.

She briskly scrubbed away all remaining evidence of the night previous, until the water ran clear.

If only it could get to her insides...

She dressed quickly, wishing she'd brought nicer clothes. When Esme had told them they were going to Vegas, she'd packed flirty-casual, not upscale elegant. And she'd thought she'd be rooming with them again, so Anj could help her do her hair while Ez consulted on makeup, just like they used to.

Maybe she just had to be okay with things never being the same again. She'd have to stand on her own.

That was the other thing they'd taught her.

When she felt sufficiently pulled together in a slouchy cowl sweater over gray leggings, she went to the interior door that opened between their room. She took a steadying breath and knocked lightly. They'd gone to bed before her, but maybe they'd stayed up chatting and were still sleeping.

There was no answer. She bit her lip as she eyed the doorknob. If they'd locked it against her, her heart would break... She turned the knob.

The door swung open, and she almost sobbed with relief.

"Anj?" she called as she stepped inside.

A note tucked into the jamb beside her head fluttered down.

Didn't want to wake u. Went down for brekkie. Text me. A.

Piper hustled back to her room for her phone. Damn, she'd forgotten to charge it last night. It died as soon as she flicked it on. She plugged it in and checked her messages. Nothing from Anj.

Morning, she typed. *Where r u guys?*

She waited, nervously pacing on the short tether of the cord, until the ding.

Morning, Pipsqueak. Down in the Badlands.

Sheesh. Seemed a little early for drinking. But whatever, at least they were talking to her. Leaving her phone to charge, she slipped into her clogs and raced to join her friends.

Before they changed their minds.

When she got there, they had a mimosa ready for her and a danish missing only one bite.

"Sorry." Anjali wrinkled her nose. "I'm supposed to be juicing, but I couldn't help myself."

Relieved that last night's awfulness seemed to have blown over, Piper grinned at her friend. "Mimosas count as juicing?"

Anj snorted. "Sure. They have orange juice, don't they?"

"True." Piper took a sip of her drink. The OJ was refreshing but so sweet. For some reason, she wanted something darker, lustier, with more bite...

Hastily, she stuffed the danish in her mouth. *This* was what she had.

After another sip of the mimosa for courage, she cleared her throat. "Guys, about last night—"

"Yeah," Anjali said. "The party next door was pretty annoying, keeping us up all night."

Piper frowned. "That *is* annoying. I guess I couldn't hear it from my side." Where she'd been banished. Not that she'd been there until much later anyway, due to her side trip to a secret underground paradise... "Uh. But I meant before that. Esme, I'm sorry about what I said about Lars. You love him, and that's what important, so I just wanted to tell you—"

"We were all tired," Anjali said.

Piper nodded but kept her gaze on Esme. "Ez?"

Her friend had been looking at her mimosa but finally raised her head. "Hmm? Sorry. I was thinking about..." She trailed off, but her brow furrowed as if she wasn't quite sure what she was going to say.

Was she still that mad? Piper bit her lip. Anj was always the one to hold a grudge, claiming her spicy temperament came from her Cajun mother. When Esme got mad, she'd explain in great detail with big words how disappointed she was that people weren't living up to their potential. She didn't do the silent treatment.

Worry about being ostracized turned to a different concern.

Piper reached across the table to touch her friend's hand, bringing her attention upward. "You okay, Ez?"

Esme's pupils were wide and jittery, as if she was having trouble focusing. Piper wondered how many mimosas she'd missed before she got there.

Anjali took Ez's other hand. "Just tired," she said again.

Piper slipped two fingers over Esme's pulse, frowning at the erratic beat. They'd had some health scares with Ez back at school, and Piper had found her first aid skills useful when working in the field. She snapped her other fingers briskly in front of Esme's nose and shook her head at the long delay before her friend blinked. "More like stoned. What did you guys do after you took off last night?"

Anj scowled at her. "We told you we were going back to the room. What did *you* do?"

Well, she wasn't going to answer that. "I think someone might've spiked Ez's drink." Piper looked at Anjali. "Are you feeling okay?"

Twin spots of color blazed on Anj's cheekbones, obvious despite the dusky cast of her skin. "I'm fine. We're fine. Maybe just tired of you calling us down."

"Tired," Ez muttered as she tilted her head back, gazing upward. She was still wearing the same winter-white sheath dress as last night except now she had a knee-length cardigan over top, and her blond hair streamed down the back in half-twisted knots. No way would she have left the room looking so unkempt. Even their pajama parties after finals had required mascara and lip gloss.

Piper widened her eyes. This was too odd. "I'm not calling you down, Anj. I really think there's something wrong with Esme. There must be an EMT on staff here, or we can get the limo to take us to a clinic in town—"

"No." Anjali reached across the table and clamped her hand on Piper's wrist.

The strange tableau—each of them linked to the other—made Piper sit back in her seat, breaking the connection.

Her hands tingled.

Probably just the champagne in the mimosa, but if there *was* something spiking the drinks, her friends could be in more trouble than she'd thought last night.

She stood up and pushed away from the table. "I don't know what's going on, but something's wrong. I'm going to get the manager."

"Piper, no." Anjali grabbed for her hand, but Piper evaded her. Esme never even glanced over at them. "You don't understand—"

She didn't. But she would.

Piper marched to the bar and summoned the bartender with more insistence than she'd ever used in her life. "Is there a manager on duty? My friend is..." What? "Sick." That should get them moving, since presumably they dealt with alcohol-induced ailments often enough to have a protocol in place.

But by the time the manager joined her and they returned to the table, Anjali and Esme were gone.

Rave's phone kept ringing even though he kept ignoring it.

The mystery of the ichor was his only concern now—

It rang again.

He grabbed it from the table with a roar. "What?"

"Mmm-Mr. Dorado? Sorry to disturb you, sir. But we have a situation."

Rave let out a slow breath. He never barked at employees.

After barking, it was too much of a temptation to bite.

"Have Torch deal with it."

"I'm really sorry, sir. But she asked specifically for you."

She?

"I'll be right there."

The call had come from the front desk manager's line, so he headed up. Not quite at a run. But, honestly, any faster and he would've been flying.

The moment he exited the elevator, his gaze latched on her. She was pacing, her arms wrapped around her middle, her dark hair flagging behind her with each turn. On her last turn, she saw him and hurried over.

Though he told himself not to touch her— everything had changed since last night—at the panic on her face, he reached out to grip her arms.

"Are you all right?" he demanded.

"No." Her voice shook, and her skin was pale over the vivid jade of her high-necked sweater. "I mean, yes, *I'm* all right. But my friends..."

"The ones who weren't at the bar last night?"

She nodded. "They're gone."

He frowned. "This is a big place—"

Her fingers clamped on his forearms, hard enough to compress the tendons there. "I was just with them. I think they might have been drugged, roofied. I went to get help, but when I came back they'd left. They aren't back in our rooms, and they aren't answering my calls."

He rolled up to the balls of his feet and growled over his shoulder to the manager, "Have Torch meet us in the security office."

He marched Piper back to the elevator. "Tell me everything."

She stuttered and stopped a few times but quickly laid out the details about her friends and their trip. "All the luggage and toiletries are in the room," she continued, "but Anj must've gone back for her purse because she didn't have it a breakfast. Usually she leaves it behind because it's this huge, heavy thing that nobody could carry. "

Her breath caught, almost a sob, and Rave felt the sound like a stab in his gut.

Even as once again he told himself not to touch her, he pulled her into his arms. "We'll find them," he promised. "If they were able to get back to the room and then head out again, they can't have been too messed up."

Piper nodded against his chest, then let out a slow breath and pulled away. She frowned, not at him but into the air. "Esme seemed worse. Anjali seemed... I don't know. Like she just didn't believe me."

"Didn't believe you, or was responsible?"

This time Piper did scowl at him. "Anj would never—"

"You told me your friend Esme is wealthy and well connected. And you said this Anjali has a history of money trouble and questionable business connections."

"That's not what I said," Piper objected. "Or not what I meant, exactly..." She looked so aghast, he wondered how she'd ever made it this far in the world.

A violent urge swept him to drag her close again, under his wing, and never let her out, never let her see the dark side.

At least not without him right there beside her.

She shook her head adamantly, black waves flying, as if rejecting the defense he couldn't offer aloud.

"This is all so confusing, but we're friends," she insisted. "Good friends."

"You said they were pushing you away last night," he reminded her. "Obviously there's more to this than you understand."

She bit her lip. "That's what Anj said."

The elevator door opened and he guided her out with a hand at the small of her back. This off-limits area was utilitarian at best, and he felt her shrink a little at the austere corridor. He needed to get some coffee into her, something warm to take the edge off her shock.

Every nerve in his body urged him to offer his own heat.

But she couldn't be his, not anymore.

And this might be his opportunity to put her in his debt.

Torch was already in the security office when they arrived. "Torch, this is Piper. Piper, my cousin Torch."

She stared up at Torch, a touch of antagonism in her stance. "We already met."

Rave shot a hard glance at his cousin. "Really."

Torch's eyes glinted. "Saw her leaving the garden passage last night."

Piper's cheeks blazed like the sconces. "Can we please find my friends?"

Torch gestured. "I have a security station open for us."

Rave quickly recapped where to start their search. With Torch expertly manning the camera feeds, they tracked Piper's friends from the lobby bar to the elevator and to their room where they disappeared inside.

Torch fast-forwarded through less than a minute of elapsed time. Then the dreadlocked friend—Anjali—stuck her head out through the door. She looked up at the hallway camera in its unobtrusive plastic bubble.

And the feed went dark.

"What?" Torch said. "No. That did not just happen."

But his quick rewind and play got the same result.

Piper leaned over the back of Torch's chair. "There are cameras in the stairwell, right? Go there."

Torch scowled over his shoulder at her but, at Rave's

raised eyebrow, did as she asked.

It was dark too.

"Follow the darkness," Rave murmured.

Torch cursed. "How did she—?"

"It doesn't matter," Piper said. "Find them."

"Below the mezzanine level, the stairwell doors are marked with fire alarms," Torch said. "They had to have exited there."

"Too many cameras to easily track," Rave said.

"Too many for her to fuck with them all," Torch said. "Hopefully."

He called up a dozen inset screens, each of them scanning four.

"There." Rave pointed. "At the Zephyr entry."

"Farthest from the Delphi wing," Torch muttered as he zoomed in. "And the busiest. Should've guessed."

Piper gripped Rave's bicep. "They're leaving. But that's not our limo. Esme's fiancé chartered a private car for us."

"Local livery," Torch said. "We should be able to get the info on it."

"We need to call the police." She looked up at Rave.

Torch snorted. "And tell them what? Two young women in town for a bachelorette party decided to drink mimosas first thing in the morning and sightsee Vegas? That's not a crime. Mostly, that's a stereotype."

Piper ignored him, her wide gaze fixed on Rave. "Something's wrong. You saw those cameras go dark. That's not by chance."

Even Torch snorted agreement at that.

Rave put his hand over hers, barely restraining his dragon at that minimal contact. "We'll figure this out. But Torch is right about the police. As odd as this looks to us, there's no overt sign of coercion or foul play. Esme gets into the cab second; Anjali doesn't push or pull her."

Piper's jaw jutted. "But—"

"Your best bet is to let us check it out for you."

She eyed him. "I'm supposed to let a casino boss place my bet for me?"

Torch snorted again, amusement this time.

Rave glared at him. "Track that cab, and let us know what you find."

He marched Piper out of the room.

She resisted, dragging her thick heels. "I want to help."

"Torch is our head of security. Let him do his job." When she opened her mouth to object, he put one finger under her jaw and gently closed it. "Sometimes what he has to do for his job isn't something other people need to see. If you want him to find your friends, leave him be."

Piper rolled her lips between her teeth, her eyes welling. "I should've let *them* be. Then they wouldn't have run."

Rave curled his hand behind her neck and gave her a little shake. "Stop. You don't know that."

"Maybe I should call Lars, or Ez's family," she fretted as if she hadn't heard him, couldn't feel his touch. "They have resources."

He shook her again until this time she looked up at him with a scowl, a touch of color finally brightening her cheeks. "*I* have resources," he reminded her. "And we're using them now. Her family and the police would start with exactly what we're doing." He frowned. "Besides, you don't seem to like them very much."

She leaned into his grasp with a ragged sigh. "I don't. But maybe it's just because I'm jealous, because Ez always had it so easy, because she has everything I don't..."

He tilted her head back to meet her lowered gaze. "You don't believe that."

After a moment, she shook her head and then she pushed him away entirely, straightening her spine. "No. I don't. I think something weird is going on, and I'm going to figure it out."

"That's my girl," he murmured.

But she wasn't his, and his dragon roared in defiance.

CHAPTER EIGHT

Piper followed Rave back to the elevator, wringing her hands. She knew there wasn't anything else she could do besides, what, run around Vegas herself? She'd have to transfer money to get back home if the private jet wouldn't take her without Esme.

A worm of unease wriggled up her back and seemed to tighten around her throat so she tugged at the cowl of her sweater. Maybe she should contact Lars anyway. She might not like him, but she knew he'd do anything to get Esme back.

Except, hadn't her whole plan for the weekend been to get Ez away from him? Well, mission accomplished, apparently.

Had that been Anjali's plan all along too?

Piper sighed and rubbed the back of her neck where the worry worm had settled in a knot.

"Turn around." Rave turned her gently away from him and put his big hands on her shoulders.

The strong pads of his thumbs dug into her tense muscles and she let out a whimper.

He froze. "Too hard?"

"Just right. Or a little to the left, actually."

"I like a woman who knows what she wants."

Did she? She'd run away from him last night with a quickness when she'd really wanted to stay.

She turned within the confines of his grasp to look up at him. "I'm so, so glad you're willing to help me," she said. "I don't know what I would've done..."

His hands flexed and released. "You don't have to wonder. I'm here."

She'd never really had that, except from Esme and Anjali. Her family loved her, but they didn't have the resources to help her. She'd busted her ass in school and at work to make sure she never needed to ask for assistance. And even with her friends, she struggled to make herself *useful* at least since she could never be their equal.

But with Rave, there was nothing she could give him that he didn't already have, no way he could want her for anything.

Except for herself.

There was something so freeing in that thought.

She leaned into his hands. "I wish there was something I could do."

"We're doing everything we can. Torch is the best you could ask for. When he finds them, we'll figure out the next step."

She nodded. "But I meant, I wish there was something I could do"—she lifted her gaze to his—"for you."

He stared down at her, his jaw flexing. What was he not saying?

The elevator door behind her dinged, and he spun her around to usher her out.

The back of her neck burned, from the tension he'd

released and from the weight of his glare. Had she
disgusted him? Annoyed him? She hadn't meant that to
sound like a proposition—well, she kind of had, but not
exactly.

He hadn't stopped her when she left last night.

He led her down a short hall to a set of double doors
and let her through. Embarrassed at his continued
silence, she took a few hurried steps away from him.
And stopped with a muffled gasp.

She hadn't realized how high they'd come, but all of
the mountains outside the city stretched before them,
stark in the harsh light of the late winter sun.

Her heart expanded at the severe desert beauty and
she found herself drawn to the window. She reached out
as if she could touch it, but at the last moment realized
she'd just leave fingerprints on the floor-to-ceiling glass.
She made a fist and set her knuckles against the
window, letting the coolness calm her fears.

"Summers in high school I worked with my dad," she
said. "I loved being outside with him. And I really enjoy
the fieldwork for my job, but I've been taking more
management tasks to pad my résumé. Sometimes I get
so crazy with all the little things that I forget to look up
and take a breath."

She was intimately aware of Rave's presence at her
shoulder. Though he didn't touch her, she felt the
radiating heat of him, and her pulse kicked up again.

"I would like to go out more too," he said gruffly.
"But there is always something that keeps me bound
here."

"Maybe..." She turned slowly toward him, setting her back to the glass. "When all this is over, maybe we could drive up to Black Mountain for the day. It's only a half hour drive or so, and I've heard the view of the Strip is great."

He looked down at her. "It is."

Her stomach clenched. "Oh. You've done it already. Of course you have. Well—"

"I could show you a secret slot canyon that opens at the end to a view, I swear, almost all the way to the Grand Canyon across some of the wildest land left in this country. Nothing but rock and sky as far as the eye can see."

A yearning note in his voice struck an answering chord in her soul, and yet he never looked out at the stunning view. Instead, his gaze was locked on her.

"You have so many secrets," she mused.

She'd meant to be teasing, but he stiffened and took a step back. "True."

He started to say something else, but his phone chimed and he half turned away to check it.

The austere sun touched him with a silvery sheen, adding metallic highlights to his thick, cocoa-brown hair. In place of the chic dress shirt he'd worn last night, a worn charcoal-gray t-shirt clung to his shoulders and biceps, showing off the faint radiance of his ink. If he worked nights, she'd probably interrupted his time off. She should count herself lucky he'd come when she asked for him.

She'd come for him again if he asked.

The chill from the glass seemed to reach out and wrap insidious tendrils around her, squeezing through her skin toward her heart. Here she was, lusting after this man, while somewhere out in that grand vista, her friends were missing. She turned away from the temptation of staring at him.

Now that she wasn't distracted by the view and he'd given her a little space, she observed the rest of the room. She'd thought it was a conference room, as wide and windowed as it was, but now she realized it was a suite like Esme's, just, oh, a hundred times more opulent.

In the foyer where they'd entered hung a triptych painting, with each of the three panels showing a mountain range and sky under divergent conditions: a peaceful morning of blue and gold, a scorching summer of red and bone-white, a storm of gray and purple. As if the wide views beyond the glass weren't enough for him.

A huge, U-shaped couch in a sunken living area at the corner convergence of the windows framed a gas fire pit—unlit at the moment—with a hanging hood, like a ski lodge on steroids. The galley kitchen beyond was all gleaming black marble and stainless steel with a wine rack and wet bar extensive enough to keep an army of après skiers drunk off their asses.

In the other direction, through a half-open door, her gaze froze on a glimpse of a gigantic bed.

Unlike the décor in the rest of the high-end suite, the bed looked positively medieval, with carved wood posters draped in dark, velvety curtains.

She had a flash of erotic imagery: her hands clutching the thick wood while Rave took her from behind...

Like her wayward thoughts, pillows had tumbled off the high mattress and lay strewn on the deep shag carpet.

So, he wasn't the sort to make his bed, but he didn't let anyone else make it either.

And apparently he'd had a rough night too.

Just like that, she remembered why she'd left him last night.

This was not her world. She didn't have secrets of her own. She wasn't rich like Ez. She wasn't an artist like Anj. She was just plain old Piper Ramirez, hard worker and frequently clueless friend.

She sidled away from Rave, trying to find a spot to stand where she didn't feel lost in the big space. "I should be out there looking for them," she fretted when he looked up from his phone.

"Torch and his people are doing everything," Rave reminded her, hefting the phone as if it were proof. "I have faith in them. We just need to give them time."

She eyed him ruefully. "If it was your friends who were lost or AWOL, would you be patient?"

Lips quirked, he inclined his head to acknowledge her point. "But if my presence was making things harder, I'd get out of the way."

She twisted her hands together, remorse corkscrewing even deeper. "I did make things worse."

He strode up to her. "This wasn't your fault. You

were worried for your friends. Rightly, it seems."

Having him so close made her want to just burrow into his arms and hide forever. But she knew that wasn't an option. Had never been, not for her. "Still, I need to do *some*thing."

"You can stay here with me, so I know you're safe," he said.

She stiffened. "Safe? What do you mean?"

"Your friends vanished under peculiar circumstances and aren't responding to calls. I don't want that to happen to you."

She wrapped her arms around herself. "No one's after me," she insisted. "Esme and Anj are the ones everybody wants."

Rave stalked a slow circle around her. "You have no idea—" Then he brought himself up short and waggled his phone. "Torch sent an update. His people went through all the security footage since your limo pulled up to the front door. There is nothing unusual—unless you count not gambling, shopping, or eating, all of which we have here in five-star abundance—until they blacked out our cameras and disappeared. They didn't talk to anyone besides you. No one approached them. Where they did have very brief interactions with staff, our employees say everything seemed fine." He finished his circle, like he was tightening a trap around her. "Whatever trouble they found, it seems they brought it with them."

Piper frowned. "Trouble? But this was just a fun little getaway with way too many spa appointments."

He eyed her. "You don't like our spas? Every woman leaves glowing reviews about our spas."

Had she hurt his feelings? Her mind spun, trying to keep up with his quicksilver moods. "I'm not every woman."

"No," he said softly. "So you aren't." His tone sharpened again. "Torch is heading to the livery company to do some of his persuading in person. Also, he sent someone to talk to the jet company and the limo driver. And he has a team looking at Esme's family and fiancé. And at Anjali. I'm betting he'll find your friends before half that intel comes back."

Piper sagged. All those people trying to help her, when she couldn't even be sure she just hadn't pissed off her friends so much they ditched her. "I won't be able to repay you."

"You won't," he agreed. "Because I won't ask you to."

She tilted her head to look up at him. "Why are you doing this?"

For a long second, she thought he wouldn't answer her. He was facing the window, and his gaze—the blue-gray of a turbulent ocean—seemed farther away than the mountain peaks.

"There is something you can do," he said. "For me."

She perked up. She worked hard to earn her merit scholarships, and she'd cleaned that college apartment bathroom more than her fair share to make up for the fact that Ez bought all the wine and ice cream and Anj scored all the weed. She never wanted to owe anyone.

"Tell me," she said.

But for all his effortless confidence, for once Rave seemed uneasy. He cast a quick glance at her before going to the window to look out. As if he didn't want to be too close to her and needed the solace of the distant view.

"I have a...malady," he said slowly, then quickly added, "It's nothing infectious or even noticeable at the moment. But..." He took a breath. "It's going to kill me. And sooner rather than later."

Piper pressed her knuckles to her lips. Her whole body angled toward him, trying to go to him, but he'd put distance between them to tell her about this, and she would honor his need for space.

"It's a degenerative condition of the blood, more or less," he continued. "I hadn't realized how far it had progressed. But last night..." He lifted his chin to meet her anguished gaze, his arms crossed hard over his wide chest. The ink on his tensed arms glinted at her, and she felt the impact of how vulnerable he was making himself to her. "Last night, I felt...alive. For the first time in a very long time." He faced her squarely. "Because of you."

She swallowed hard. "Because of...what we did."

"The sex, yes," he said bluntly. "But it was more than that. We have a connection." His gaze sharpened. "You felt it too."

She should bristle at being told what she'd felt. Especially considering he'd let her leave without a single word. Never mind that she hadn't *let* him speak.

But she had to admit, he wasn't wrong.

At just the thought of what they'd done, a wisp of

heat unfurled inside her, like the geothermal springs welling up from secret places under the Keep. How terrible was she, to be intrigued by him with her friends missing. But he was helping her find them, so surely that deserved some sort of prize.

Or maybe she shouldn't be so coy about it: it was a payment for services rendered, sex for security, handing over her chips for a chance to roll his dice...

Okay, now she was being ridiculous.

"I felt it," she admitted. "It scared me. That's why I left."

With a sharp breath, he strode toward her, taking her arms. "I never meant to scare you, Piper."

She looked up at him with a wry smile. "Like, by charging at me and grabbing me?"

His hands sprang open and he veered away, then he shot her a wary, sidelong glance. "Are you teasing me?"

"A little. It's the only defense I have against you, I guess."

"I don't want you to have anything against me." He circled around her again, a slow stalk. "Except your body."

With one last hopeful thought for her friends and a prayer that Rave's people could find them, Piper gave herself up to this second chance.

She turned to face him, stopping his restless spiral with one hand on his chest, right above where she knew that blank spot was under the gray t-shirt, unmarked by any tattoos.

"Tell me what you felt," she murmured.

His chest heaved on a deep breath. "My skin had grown cold. My nerves no longer responded to pain. Or pleasure. Sometimes my joints ache so badly, I don't move for days. But last night, your heat melted it all away, reshaped the ache to something sweeter, like wine flowing through my veins. Your laughter filled the hollowness in my bones. I want that again. I want you..."

Her fingers curled in his shirt, wrinkling the soft fabric, and she swayed toward the longing in his voice.

"I've never been that, not to anyone." She splayed her hand wide, feeling the urgent pounding of his heart. Maybe she was being naïve to believe him; no man alive spoke like that, but... "I want that too."

He closed the half step between them and swept her off her feet, one arm behind her shoulders, his elbow crooking under her knees.

She knew his strength now and so she didn't make a sound at the abrupt change of altitude, only buried her face in his neck, inhaling the spicy mineral scent of his skin.

He strode to the bedroom, wheeling her easily through the wide doorway, and kicked the door closed behind them.

Here too the windows were floor to ceiling, filled only with stark winter light, but the bed dominated the room, promising dark and lush temptations.

Rave let her legs slide down, leaving her kneeling on the bed. The thick mattress sank under her weight but was still so high that for once, she was a little taller than him.

She kept her arm looped around his neck and buried her fingers in his dark hair while she stared down at him hungrily.

"Now," she said, "*show me* what you felt."

CHAPTER NINE

By all the skies, she was everything a dragon could desire: innocent and bold, strong yet yielding. And so damn sexy.

Rave skimmed his hands under the long hem of her sweater and up over the curve of her hips to sink his fingers into the padded flesh of her ass. *So* damn sexy.

He dragged his hand back up her body, snagging her sweater at the same time. She raised her hands to let him strip it over her head, then raked her fingers through his hair, tilting his head back and leaning down to kiss him.

Her mouth was open, hot, all but breathing the fever of her arousal. The dragon within him fought his restraints and rose, twisting, all of his muscles tightening with its ravenous urge to devour her.

If she didn't swallow him whole first.

Her full lips streaked across his, wet and slick, her tongue flicking down to tantalize him, her hunger as wild as his.

His despair was close behind. How could she hope to match his dragon's cravings when she didn't even know it existed, would never believe his story?

But she *had* believed him when he told her— obliquely, yes, but truthfully—about the petralys that would kill him. She artlessly accepted his halting explanation, her heart as pure and open as the waters of the garden pool even when she'd admitted he scared her.

Well, she fucking *terrified* him.

If she was one of the near-mythical solarys, how could he ever let her go?

Her fingers tightened almost painfully in his hair, cranking his head back to break the kiss.

She stared down at him. "You were going cold on me again, weren't you?"

"Never," he murmured. He grasped her arms behind her back, forcing her to arch toward him. Her breasts swelled lusciously, the shadowed rounds of her areolas darkening the pale, silky fabric of her bra. He ducked his head and with a clamp of his jaws unlatched the clasp between her breasts. The halves split apart like a fragile eggshell, revealing the lavish mounds.

He laved his tongue across one dusky nub and drew it into a dark, shining peak, bright with her rushing blood. By the time he turned his attention to her other nipple, sucking it high, like an erotic echo of the mountain range out the window behind her, she was writhing against him, her breath coming in mewling gasps.

"So beautiful," he murmured. Her body reminded him of the triptych in the entry—land and sky revealing so many moods that despite all his centuries, he could never grow weary of the sight. "So willing."

Her hands fisted in his shirt, a wordless demand. He was willing too and let her strip the shirt from him.

For all his half nakedness, his skin flushed hot under her dark eyes, glazed with desire.

He wasn't just willing; he was dying for her.

He stalked up her onto the bed, tumbling her onto her back and stripping off her leggings and panties with trembling hands. He might've feared that the stone blight had him in its grasp, but this wasn't a distant, frozen pain. This was the burning agony of his need to have her, here, now.

Her hands were equally frantic on his jeans, yanking the fly wide with an urgency that made him wince for fear of his tender bits while that same vulnerable flesh was eagerly bursting out into her grasp.

She stroked him once as he clambered over her, finally naked, and it was all he could do not to orgasm in her curious fingers. He pumped his hips with a groan, and she answered with a softer moan.

He grabbed both her wrists in one hand and stretched her wide on the big bed, arms above her head, legs splayed as he pushed his knees between her thighs.

She wriggled impatiently, but he tightened his grip, staring down at her.

"I would find your friends for you anyway," he said.

"I would fuck you anyway," she countered.

With that attitude, how could he *not* be drawn to her? He dipped his head to ravish her mouth. As she'd teased him, now he took his revenge until she was undulating beneath him, the hard points of nipples stabbing his chest every time she arched up.

If she wasn't careful, she was going to impale herself

on his rampant cock. Since she seemed insensible to the danger, he took matters—and his dick—into his own hands and reached over to the bedside table to fumble for a condom. He'd never understood why Torch insisted that all dragonkin keep "protection" close at hand—he'd never needed it. For a century he hadn't even bothered wondering what kind of sword went in this particular sheath. But now he fervently apologized for doubting his cousin. His dragon might not be able to catch or spread any human diseases, but if this simple barrier eliminated the need to explain all that, then good enough.

Piper smiled at him, giving him a peek of her gaped teeth. So she *had* been aware of the need for a condom, and she'd waited for him to do the right thing for her. Her trust nearly destroyed him.

Especially when he thought of why he was really doing this.

But for all his self-disgust, his cock swelled to epic proportions as he edged between her thighs. She feathered her fingers up his pecs and then over his shoulders, instinctively following the flow of flight muscles that strained for release even in this earthbound form.

She clasped him closer while spreading her legs, the long bones of her thighs gently padded to welcome him as he centered himself at her opening.

Her slick, wet folds parted at his touch, more precious to him than the golden gates that guarded his subterranean garden. As he nudged the thick head of his cock into her depths, she threw back her head. Against his wine-dark sheets, her glossy black hair made standing waves, like shining volcanic obsidian. She was everything fiery and flowing, her hidden inner muscles clenching around him as if she'd never let him go and then releasing just enough to take him deeper.

His breath grew rough with holding himself back, swallowing the dragon's hungry rumble. She would hear the beast, she would know—on some level—what he was. He couldn't let that happen, not when he needed her willing surrender in the hopes of subverting her solarys energy to revitalize the ichor.

He clamped his teeth hard and drove into her with renewed urgency.

She matched him, thrust for thrust, her fingers gliding down his spine to grip his ass. She spread his butt cheeks wide with the force of her clenching fingers, and the tickle of air across that rarely exposed part of himself made him pound helplessly into her pussy.

She cried out, and aghast that he might have hurt her, he tried to pull back, but she bowed off the bed, her hips grinding hard on his pelvis as she came in an explosive rush.

Unable—unwilling—to control himself, he tumbled after her.

And the dragon's hoarse scream of triumph ripped from his throat.

His shout made her come again. Piper closed her eyes as every muscle seized in agony and ecstasy, lightning cascading through her pussy and shooting out along every nerve until her fingers and toes were tingling.

Rave thrust again and again, riding the waves of their reverberating orgasm, and each aftershock made her gasp, silver and gold sparkles exploding behind her eyelids.

What the hell had he done to her? She never came so easily, at least not with anyone else. It was as if he knew her body as well as she did after only one—two, now—encounters.

God, what would she give him for a third shot? Everything, probably.

As soon as she thought it, the possibility disturbed her. A one-night stand was one thing. An afternoon quickie in the unflinching light of day was another. But third times...

Well, that was always the charm, wasn't it?

He was still braced above her on stiffened arms, his chest heaving and his head hanging down so his forehead touched her crown. The gusts of his breath ruffled her hair, sending a fresh shiver down her spine and goosebumps trailing after.

He touched every part of her even when he wasn't touching her.

She looked down at their joined bodies, how he pierced her to the quick, but was more achingly aware of their harmonized breath, in and out, gradually slowing.

And still his powerful arms held him just above her.

She flattened her palm over the empty skin above his heart, her spread fingers not quite an X-marks-the-spot.

"It's like a treasure map," she mused.

If she hadn't been so attuned to their breath, she might not have noticed the way his caught in surprise.

"A what?"

"A treasure map. See, here's the mountains. Here's the woods." She feathered her fingers through the dusting of hair on his chest and grinned at him. "Here's a coastline and river. Even the skull and crossbones. All these tattoos are little clues leading us to the buried pirate booty." She reached down to squeeze his butt.

With a grunt, he finally collapsed his arms, thumping down on the mattress beside her. He slipped out of her and rolled away to discard the condom.

She traced a finger over the tattoos that continued across his shoulder blades. "Maybe you could get one that says 'Here be dragons.'"

He muttered something.

"What?"

He rolled back to face her, bending one arm under his head. "I said, pirates aren't the only ones with buried treasure."

She curled her arm into a pillow, mirroring his stance. "I suppose you know all about booty in a casino."

He blinked slowly. "Are we still talking about money or backsides?"

"Both, I guess. It's just... It seems to me you have

everything anyone could ever want here, all the money, all the excitement, but you don't seem..." She bit her lip.

This was where she'd gotten into trouble with Esme and Anjali, judging Ez's relationship with Lars, mentioning Anj's lack of relationship with anyone. She'd driven them away with her pestering; she wasn't going to make that same mistake with Rave.

His brow furrowed, not in anger, more questioning. "I don't seem what?"

"Never mind." She blushed. "I blame my work, where I take little samples of things and try to figure out what's inside them. I don't know you well enough to know what you are or aren't."

"Oh, I think you might know more than you know," he said cryptically. "I've shown you more than I've ever shown anyone."

"The garden is amazing. And the waterfall. The wine was amazing." She couldn't stop herself from reaching out to run her fingers through his tousled hair. "*You* are amazing."

It wrecked her to consider whatever condition was slowly killing him. She didn't want to imagine a world without his keen, passionate intensity. From his vague description, she thought his issue might be some sort of neurodegenerative disorder, stealing his ability to feel and move. The symptoms were so contrary to the vibrant man beside her, it simply wasn't right.

"I'm not amazing." He caught her hand and held her fingers to his cheek. "I'm cursed. And all the riches and thrills of this place won't change that."

She could almost believe the truth of that word. "I was going to say you seem lonely."

"Another way to say what I said."

"Maybe you just haven't found the right someone to be with yet."

He turned her hand over and pressed a kiss to the pulse point in her wrist. "And maybe I have."

She knew he must have felt the sudden burst of her blood raging under his lips. "Rave…"

"Piper, would you stay? If I asked you—if I said please and thank you and all the other words people say—would you stay and try to save me as you want to save your friends?" His stony-stormy eyes seemed to swirl with mysterious clouds, hiding lightning in their depths.

"Stay? Here?" She almost stuttered the words. "You mean tonight?"

"I mean stay with me. Forever." His lips brushed her wrist again, not a kiss this time but with a mocking smile. "Although with me, forever probably won't be very long."

Her mind raced even faster than her pulse. Why would he even ask her to stay? She wasn't anyone, wasn't any*thing* to him. He could have anyone he asked for. Well, maybe not Esme and Anjali since they'd run away. But anyone else.

But he was here, with her, right now.

She opened her mouth, not sure herself what she was going to say, but he abruptly leaned forward and kissed her, swallowing her response.

"Hold that thought," he said. "I'll be right back."

He spun off the bed, dropping easily to the floor off the high mattress in another scattering of pillows. The firm globes of his butt flexed as he bent to scoop up a couple of the pillows and toss them back to her with a smile. For someone with a supposedly painful and debilitating condition, he seemed all right at the moment...

She frowned to herself as he padded away to the bedroom's other doorway and flicked on a light that illuminated the dark marble tiles of a bathroom. He closed the door on her semi-suspicious stare, and she heard the sound of water running.

It wasn't that she doubted him. Exactly. But she knew he had secrets—she'd already seen some of them—and she couldn't have uncovered all of them in only a day. Even if she had uncovered all of *him*.

Like the map of tattoos across his body, she suspected there was a lot more to see if she just looked at him in the right light.

She rolled onto her back, staring up at the canopy of the bed. She angled her head a bit to study the carved wood poster holding up the heavy drapes. At first she thought the posters were etched with the standard ivy leaves or some such, but when she looked closer, she realized they were scales. Twining serpents climbed up the poles and snaked across the headboard. No, not snakes. Spines and wings flared over the canopy, and forked tongues seemed to angle down to flicker at her.

No wonder she'd been thinking "here be dragons".

She didn't mind scaled things. When she was out in the field taking water samples, she encountered plenty of fish, frogs, and small water snakes, and she liked seeing them since healthy critters usually meant healthy water.

Still, the design seemed strangely sensuous and profane for what was clearly a well-worn antique.

It fit Rave perfectly.

She sighed. What was she going to tell him when he returned? They'd had sex twice and known each other less than one day. That wasn't enough to base a relationship on, was it? And then there was the whole thing with her missing friends...

She shook her head restlessly against the sheets. She was just going to have to tell him they needed to slow down.

Except she knew he didn't have that kind of time—

He emerged from the bathroom, striding toward her.

His jaw was set in a determined line, and blood dripped down from the crook of his arm, bright as flames.

CHAPTER TEN

His mind made up, Rave waited until his pupils had gone from the dragon's slitted stare to a more human circle before he exited the bathroom. "Piper, there's something I need to tell you—"

"Oh my god, Rave!"

She bolted from the bed and ran toward him. She'd grabbed a bolster from the bed on the way, and for a second he thought they were going to have some sort of porn-tastic pillow fight. But then she stripped the case and reached for his arm.

"What happened?" She lifted his elbow, catching the stream of blood in the pillow case and wrapping the fabric tight, but not too tight. "Are you hurt anywhere else?"

"It's nothing," he said impatiently. Lately, excising ichor had been like digging for buried treasure, except the treasure was halfway to China and only half a gold coin. He hadn't expected to find it so fast and close to the surface this time. The iron knife he'd stuck in his arm had melted and shocked him at the same time when it touched the ichor surging wildly just beneath his skin, and he'd been so surprised he cut himself more deeply than he thought.

And then he'd come running to find her.

"It's not nothing," she argued. "That's going to need

stitches. You're not hurt anywhere else?"

"No. I..." What? Cut himself shaving? She wasn't going to believe that. And anyway, he needed to tell her the truth—more of the truth, at least—if he was going to prepare her to be a solarys.

To save Bale.

He let out a slow breath. "I was checking my blood." No sense trying to explain ichor right away.

She frowned. "Like glucose monitoring? No test needs that much blood outside of a collection tube."

"I slipped." He tried a smile at her.

But she was having none of it. "Who is your doctor? If we need to get you seen—"

"Nobody needs to see me." Except her. She was going to save his liege and give the Nox Incendi a stay of execution.

Her expression softened. "It must be hard for you. Admitting you need help in this when you have so much power everywhere else."

He shook his head. "I can say it. I need your help, Piper. My people will find your friends, but I need you to help me."

She looked up at him, her dark eyes luminous above the jade of her sweater. "I'm here for you."

So simple, so naïve. No wonder dragons ate innocents.

He was going to tear her world apart to save his.

"Come with me." He wiped the worst of the gore from his arm and tossed the pillow case away before reaching for her clothes.

"Rave. You need to keep pressure on that—"

He unfolded his bare arm toward her, flexing just enough to show her the ragged edges of the careless cut he'd made.

The edges already knitting together.

She closed her eyes. Then looked again. "What?" Her voice was faint.

"I know you have questions." He handed her clothing over. "But it will be easier to just show you. Will you come?"

She didn't answer but she got dressed, casting sidelong glances his way as he did the same, yanking on his jeans, t-shirt, and boots.

He took her down deep to his laboratory. In the elevator, she lifted his arm in her hands, turning it under the light. The filaments of new flesh webbing the wound were tenuous, stretching with her tentative exploration, but there was no more blood.

She made a soft sound of confusion but didn't otherwise speak.

He didn't blame her.

His own mind was racing with how he would explain, how he would win her cooperation. And what he would do if the first two failed.

As they walked into his lab, she made another sound and rocked back in her clogs. She was a scientist too, of course, so he knew she'd recognize some of the equipment. But many of his tools and processes had been taken from the ancient alchemists, and the alembics, crucibles, mortars, and cast-iron cauldron had a distinctly medieval cast.

Not to mention the knightly suit of steel armor.

With the giant bite taken out of it.

Her gaze went around and around before settling back on him.

"What is this place?"

"Where I'm trying to cure this disease."

"You're a casino mafia boss *and* a doctor? And an *Antiques Roadshow* fan?"

He grunted. "None of those. I'm..." The truth beat inside him with powerful wings. But he'd restrained that beast for a long time. "I'm the closest to an answer that I've ever been. Because of you." He guided her toward the work bench.

He handed her the crystal flask with Bale's moribund ichor lumped at the bottom. He tried to see it with her untaught eyes, and even so he thought it must seem like what it was: death. "There is a substance in my blood that used to look something like this. Not quite this ominous, but nearly."

She raised the flask to the light, turning it slowly. "Some sort of heavy metal contaminant?"

He blinked. Untaught, maybe, but not stupid. "Something like that."

"You tried chelation? The proper binding agent would depend on the pollutant, of course." She trailed off. "But if you've been studying this, I'm sure you tried everything already."

"I thought I had," he said. "I admit, I hadn't considered binding and extraction." Removing the ichor entirely would kill the dragon.

But maybe it would save the man.

He shook his head. A dragon-shifter was nothing without his beast. "Chelation won't work. The substance is actually a key component of our blood."

"Our?"

Shit. This was already getting complicated. He didn't want to expose the existence of the rest of the Nox Incendi if he didn't have to.

But she'd at least be meeting Bale.

If she was to become the king's mate.

Rave's dragon lashed inside him, but he forced it down, as he'd done time and time again for the good of the tribe. "My brother suffers from the same disorder, although his case is more advanced than mine."

Piper lowered the flask and met his gaze. "What do you think I can do? My expertise is water quality, which is a health issue, but not with direct human applications."

Well, he wasn't human anyway. He swallowed that response. "I told you when we were together last night I felt...different. More alive."

Her lips twisted wryly to one side. "I thought it was a come-on."

He scowled at her. "I'd be so unoriginal?"

"Well, sorry, I didn't know you then."

As if she did now.

He choked on that thought too. "It was a real change. Watch." He unfurled his arm in front of her, displaying the nearly healed cut. "Compared to the sample in the beaker, my blood was almost as compromised. But now—" He revealed the scalpel in his other hand.

"Rave!" She jolted toward him.

So bold. He hadn't expected her to react that quickly, so he cut with more urgency than precision. Tracing the line he'd made before, but not so deep, he released the ichor.

The dragon responded to the wound even faster than Piper. Translucent, rainbowed ichor flowed up into the wound, sparking.

Piper jumped back with a yelp. The scalpel melted, and he dropped it before his fingers singed.

The ichor sank back below his skin, with a hiss and a faint whiff of scorched metal. The fresh cut bled for a moment before sealing over.

Piper didn't try to staunch the bleeding this time.

A twinge of disappointment made him tighten his jaw. He'd shocked her... But then he saw she was staring hard at the wound, brow furrowed in concentration.

"It's real," she murmured. "Not a special effect."

Hell. Wait until she saw the dragon...

"It's real."

"What do you call it?"

"Ichor. It's an inherited trait with my tribe." As soon as he said tribe, he realized he was revealing too much, but she seemed to take the word as given.

"Everyone who inherits the...ichor eventually suffers the degeneration?"

He hesitated. "Yes. The malady is called petralys."

"Petra," she muttered. "Means stone. The initial sample looked like it's turning to stone."

"It is." He'd been over this himself a thousand times—more than a thousand—but for some reason, this time it didn't feel hopeless. Other dragonkin had tried to help, but he'd always been alone in this task. Not anymore. He saw the wheels turning behind her dark, thoughtful eyes.

"So what made you suspect having sex with me would cure you?"

He stiffened. Was that a thread of hurt in her voice? "Nothing. I didn't know there'd be any effect. I...I was drawn to you. And we... Only later, when I took a sample of my blood, I saw the change."

"Mm-hmm. So you decided today to see if you could replicate the results."

Oh, that was definitely a note of censure.

And he knew it was only going to get worse.

"We can help each other," he reminded her. "We both have something the other needs."

She glanced away from him then back. "Right. So you find my friends, and I help you and your brother. You have a security team, and I have... What am I supposed to do?"

"I don't know," he admitted. "I wondered if it was merely your presence. But the decaying ichor in the flask isn't reacting."

"Maybe I have to be in contact with it." She averted her gaze. "We touched. A lot."

The dragon roared a challenge. It would never let

her touch another.

Rave managed to restrain the sound, only shook his head curtly. "Except in the rare instances of me slashing myself open, the ichor is confined by my flesh, rather like the sample is contained in the crystal. It didn't need to have direct physical contact to react to you."

She pursed her lips. "Your flesh—hard body though you are—isn't impermeable as the crystal is." She reached for the stopper.

He put his hand over hers, and she looked up at him.

Did he feel something inside when he touched her? Was that her solarys power? Or was it just his exquisite awareness of everything about her: the determined set of her shoulders, the daring gleam in her dark eyes, her scent—raw honey and cinnamon. And the lingering perfume of their lovemaking.

She tilted her head. "Why are you hesitating now?"

Because he didn't want to risk her. For her sake and for his brother's life.

And for his own.

If he lost her...

As if she sensed the corrosive doubt, worse than the stone blight, holding him hostage, she wriggled her hand under his, loosening the crystal stopper.

He tensed, ready to knock the flask out of her hand if Bale's ichor erupted with the same ferocity as his.

But the blackened lump might as well have been at the bottom of the ocean.

She peered into the flask, huffing a breath over the

opening, and gave it a swirl.

Nothing.

She frowned. "Maybe it's all correlative, no causation."

"No. I know there was a reaction. I saw it. I *felt* it."

The look she gave him was almost pitying. "I know how much this means to you—"

"Not just to me," he snapped. "To every male in my tribe."

Her eyes widened. "It's not just your brother and you?"

He dragged his hands through his hair. Everything was spiraling out of his control. "All the males are affected. About a hundred, all told."

She capped the flask and gave it back to him. "But not the females? Maybe it's genetic or hormonal. Although there could be environmental factors. If we compare—"

"There are no females in our line."

She blinked. "What? Did you all hatch parthenogenetically?"

He felt his cheeks redden. "Not exactly."

She interlaced her fingers behind her head, holding tight as if to keep her blown mind together. "This is just too bizarre. I can't even... I don't know what I expected to happen."

"Well, you came to Las Vegas for a girls' night out. Presumably you expected to take some chances, lose more than you could really afford, and make some questionable choices that you wouldn't have to talk about once you left here."

She blinked again. "Check, check, and check."

Which one was he?

The thought stabbed him more deeply than the scalpel had, and what welled up wasn't the opalescent fury of the ichor but something from his bones: an awareness that it was going to kill him to let her go.

And not just literally.

His phone rang, the discordant interruption jangling his temper. He stabbed the slide. "Torch. Piper is here with me. What have you found?"

After the briefest pause, where Rave suspected his cousin adjusted whatever he'd been about to blurt out based on the audience, Torch said, "Talked to the cab driver. He says he was waiting in the stand and was next in line when the women approached. He didn't know them. He said the red-haired one asked to go to the Strip. There was no conversation on the way there. They paid in cash. He didn't note which way they went."

"And from there they could've gone anywhere." Rave avoided looking at Piper.

"Haven't found the limo driver that brought them originally. The vehicle is from a local livery, but their paperwork is...sketchy. The contact on the rental papers isn't answering the phone number he provided, but the car was paid for with a credit card issued to Ashcraft Amalgamated—"

"That's Esme's fiancé's company," Piper cut in. "Based out of Salt Lake."

"The jet is registered to them too," Torch continued.

"I have someone watching the plane, but it seems to be locked down for now. No flight plan has been filed. And the pilot isn't answering at the number he left on record with the airfield manager."

Piper muttered under her breath. "Is everyone missing?"

Rave rubbed his jaw. "Are they all together or are Ashcraft's people looking for your friends too?"

"Lars would be out here in a minute with all his resources if he knew Esme wasn't where he'd scheduled her to be," Piper said. "Maybe we should tell him—"

"Let's hold off on that," Torch said. "Your little friend Anjali is leading us on, but I think I'm getting a sense of her wiles."

"But you said Anj took them to the Strip," Piper said. "That one street just by itself is too huge to search."

"Yes, isn't it." Torch drawled the words. "She likes darkness and she likes chaos. I can work with that."

Rave heard the sound of the provoked predator in his cousin's voice: with Torch, the lazy eyeroll of a bored, lounging hunter could shift in a heartbeat to a deadly pounce.

Piper's friend wouldn't stay lost for long, and then she'd regret attracting the attention of a barely civilized dragon-shifter with a penchant for havoc.

"Anyway," Torch said more briskly. "I'm just calling to find out what level of persuasion is authorized."

"By any means necessary," Rave said.

"Well, don't scare them," Piper objected.

Torch snorted. "Sweetheart, that don't even move

the needle."

The line disconnected.

Piper looked at Rave uncertainly. "I don't know about this. I don't know about any of this."

Her confusion and concern was like a fist squeezing his chest. But he knew she'd never be more amenable to coercion.

"Torch will do anything to finish his mission," he told her. "Until then, I want to take you to meet my brother."

She was so distracted by what was going on with her friends, she didn't even question him.

But as they took the private elevator to the highest floor of the Keep, with each story they rose, he hammered himself with doubts and his heart plunged in a death spiral.

CHAPTER ELEVEN

She knew they'd been underground, and she knew the Keep was almost a skyscraper and they were heading to the top, but she felt like they were in the elevator forever.

Or maybe that was just her thoughts and fears trapped in an endless rollercoaster of up and down. She'd gone from her quiet microscope in a boring beige office building to this outlandish fever dream of weirdness.

Friends gone missing. Bizarre blood disorders. A mysterious stranger who roused in her a desire that was morphing into an addiction.

She remembered her father telling her, "Pick the fruit in front of you. Wait for the ones that will be ripe tomorrow."

He hadn't been offering any particular kind of wisdom. He'd just been talking about apples and cherries, but she thought it still applied.

Abruptly Rave said, "Please don't be afraid of...of my brother. With the petralys condition, light and heat are painful. He's been confined to these rooms for...awhile."

Piper nodded, touched by his urge to defend his brother. "I dealt with my dad's illness," she reminded him. "And in my job, I've identified toxic algae blooms and brain-eating amoebas and parasitic infestations that cause deformations in fish and frogs. I don't startle easy."

Never mind how often she'd gasped since getting out of that stupid limo.

Rave swayed from one boot to the other. "Bale is a...a little larger than any of those."

The elevator door chimed quietly.

And opened to utter blackness.

"Uh," she said.

The hesitant breath whispered out into the void and seemed to be swallowed.

"Rave." A voice came out of the dark. "What have you done?"

Rave stepped out of the elevator. "I found a solarys."

What was a solarys? Was it something to help his brother? Why hadn't Rave told her about it when they were discussing cures?

Piper took a short step toward Rave, peering into the shadows. The light from behind her fell on the floor, illuminating bare cement, but reached no farther into the room beyond. She knew they must be in the penthouse, but the mineral tang of cold, wet stone reminded her unnervingly of her father's funeral and the raw, gaping hole in the earth. She stopped on the verge between the elevator car and the concrete, preventing the door from closing.

From the dark came a low, rasping sigh. "With the solarys, you will rule the Nox Incendi."

Piper wedged her foot against the elevator door that was trying to push her out of the way. Nox...what?

Incendi? Did he mean the chemical term NOx? The dangerous atmospheric compounds formed during high-temp combustion, like lightning strikes. She'd always struggled with the Latinate names in her biology classes, but nox meant night or something. Nox incendi...burning night?

And Rave would rule it with this solarys thing?

What. The. Hell.

Okay, she might've sort of lied to Rave. She didn't startle easily, but she was *done* with mysteries. Time to hit the bar downstairs.

She sidled back a step. And now of course the elevator door decided not to close right away.

Without looking back, Rave reached for her wrist and tugged her to his side.

"She is not my solarys, Bale," he said, still facing the darkness. "She is for you."

She? Meaning... *Qué chingados.* That meaning was clear enough.

She yanked her hand out of his hold.

But the door slid silently shut behind her, casting them into unrelenting blackness.

Unrelenting except for the very faintest spark of color hovering in the darkness.

No, not one spot. Two.

Red.

Eyes.

She shrank against Rave's shoulder, not startled, pretty much just damn terrified. She wanted to push him away furiously—*she is for you*, forget that—but he was the only thing she could hold onto in the void. Her heart skittered madly, as if it was going to find a way out, away from this Bale, with or without her.

There was no way out of this lightless place.

She swallowed hard, forcing her wimpy heart back into place. "What..." No, that sounded too weak. "Rave, I promised to help you. This is starting to feel like...something else."

Rave didn't reply. She couldn't even hear him breathing or feel his heat, though all her other senses were on high alert in this blindness; it was as if he'd turned to stone.

But the voice in the darkness answered, "Sacrifice."

Piper recoiled from the hissed word. "I didn't agree to that, no way."

"Not your sacrifice. His."

Finally, Rave let out a noise, a pained huff as if he'd been punched in the belly. "I must. Your life is worth more than mine, brother."

Though she couldn't see his face, she heard the anguish in his voice.

And she knew what that felt like, too well. Even though he'd betrayed her, she couldn't let the statement stand.

"No one's life is worth more than another's," she snapped. She hadn't always believed that. The daughter of an immigrant farm worker couldn't help but absorb some brutal lessons along with the smell of nitrogen and phosphorous. And living in the shadows of rich, elegant Esme and spirited, alluring Anjali hadn't taught her much different. But she knew better now.

"Maybe in your world," Rave rasped. "But the king of the Nox Incendi comes first."

King? Her mind reeled at this new revelation. Certainly the name and the décor of the Keep was strangely medieval, but they couldn't have an actual king. Even mafias only had godfathers, right?

Those red eyes blinked. "I know the sacrifices you've made for me, Rave, to keep me here. I know you'd give your life for mine."

Despite the shivers that racked her at the seething, inhuman glitter, Piper stepped in front of Rave. "No. There's another way."

"There is *no* way." Bale's voice was tinged not so much with regret as weariness. "Let it go, brother. Let. Me. Go."

"But I finally found her," Rave argued. "A true mate that can reignite the ichor. That can save—"

"She is not a solarys," Bale countered. "She is *your* solarys. Do you not understand the difference?"

This had gone too damn far. Despite her utter confusion and the intimidating darkness, Piper whirled and held her flattened palms out to both men. "Stop!" She managed not to shriek, but it was a close thing. "Just stop. You're making me a pawn in some game I don't understand, and I won't let you."

A ragged laugh from the shadows. "Your kind have always been game to us."

She scowled in his direction. "What is a...solarys?"

Rave answered this time. "The petralys turns us to

stone. A solarys is the numinous light and the heat that counteracts it."

She frowned. "But you said *I* am a solarys. Is it a person or a power or..."

"All of those things," Bale said. "But only to your true mate."

"Mate?" Her outstretched hands fell to her sides with a hollow clap.

Off to one side, a candle ignited, so bright after the darkness that Piper had to shield her eyes, dazzled.

In that first flare, though, she'd seen something. Something larger than a man. Something that reflected the tiny flame with more than skin's brightness.

Something...otherworldly.

By the time she peered out again, the presence had retreated from the light. The small circle of illumination didn't reach beyond the low hump of damp stone it was sitting on—what kind of penthouse was this?—but it was enough for her to see Rave.

She blinked at him angrily. "I promised to help you and then you didn't tell me *anything*? Why not just continue on as you'd been going, alone and failing, if that's how you wanted to play it?"

In the flickering light, he dipped his dark head. "You're right."

She drew a breath, ready to keep haranguing him, but his acknowledgment deflated her. "Yeah, I am."

Another grating chuckle from Bale. "Quite the prize you've found, brother."

She shot a narrow-eyed glare in the direction of the

lurking shape she could almost but not quite make out. "I'm no one's prize."

"Sharper than Damascus steel, more precious than gems," Bale said. "Clearly a pain in the ass."

Rave peered past the candle, as if he could actually see his brother. "Do you feel anything? I noticed a...difference in her presence immediately, but it wasn't until I sampled my ichor that I was sure. If you would let me draw your blood—"

"No," Bale said.

"Or we could take a draw from Piper, and try a transfusion—" Desperation quickened Rave's words.

"Why don't you just tell me to fuck him?" Piper snarked. "That's what we actually did."

He swung toward her, his lip curling in a snarl. The expression transformed his face into something bestial, sending a spasm of fear down her spine that tried to twist her legs into mindlessly fleeing. She refused, glaring at him.

Bale's distinctive rasping chuckle broke their furious but frozen tableau. "Do it, Rave," he mocked. "Command her to fuck me. To save my life. To bring her friends back. If I had my full power, I could take this city apart and you'd both have what you want."

Could Bale find Esme and Anjali? Piper averted her gaze from Rave, but from his stricken expression, she decided he at least must believe that his brother could do as he said.

Piper wrapped her arms around her middle. She was deathly worried for Esme's well-being and baffled by

Anjali's unwillingness to see the problem. But she wasn't going to sleep with a stranger to figure it out.

Other than the stranger she'd already slept with, of course.

Was she?

Was there really an unusual substance in her that interacted with the ichor in Rave and kept him alive? She clamped her arms tighter around herself, as if she might feel whatever it was. Even though it was hard to believe. But then, she frequently had her eyeballs pressed to a microscope that could see things no one else would believe present in an otherwise clear drop of water. Interdependence and atomic resonance and the placebo response were all scientific principles she'd studied and didn't deny.

Would she deny these Nox Incendi a chance at life?

The cold of the concrete floor had crept up her legs, chilling her skin, but she found herself looking to Rave again.

He didn't get a say in what she did with her body. *She'd chosen* to go with him last night and again today. And *only* she got to choose what happened between her legs.

And yet somehow—when had *this* happened?—he apparently got some sort of say about what happened in her heart.

If he tried to hand her over to his brother, his king, whatever, he was going to break her heart.

Why had she given him that power?

But she knew that wasn't the way it worked, any

more than he had given her the power to somehow affect the ichor that flowed in his veins.

It just *was*, like the hydrogen bond of frozen water molecules turned ice into the perfect symmetry of a snowflake.

If there'd been a door anywhere she could see—hell, even a window—she would've left rather than wait for *his* choice. She'd made it a point to never confront anyone about her worth, for fear she'd be found wanting. The one time she'd questioned Esme and Anjali, they'd left her behind.

And now she was forced to watch Rave weighing the value of her heart.

When he didn't even know that's what he had in his hands.

CHAPTER TWELVE

It killed him. No, Bale should kill him for the traitor that he was.

But Rave could not relinquish his true mate. Not for his brother, not for his king, not for the good of all the Nox Incendi.

She was his.

With a rumbling growl, he pulled her to his side, though she resisted mightily. He glared across the guttering candle that even with its feeble light and warmth must be agony to Bale. The stone blight would end him, and yet it was Rave's fault.

With his roused dragon's keen eyesight, he caught a glimpse of his brother, more than he'd had in several years. The petralys had advanced in that time, leaving Bale half shifted. The bare skin visible through his ragged clothes was hardened with thick scales, and draconic spines bristled along his backbone. But his wings were gnarled, as if they'd been broken.

Had he thrown himself against the concrete walls of his voluntary cage? He would never fly again with those wings.

The truth ripped through Rave.

His brother would never fly again regardless.

"You can't give her away," Bale said, his voice caught halfway between envy and awe. "Even if you wanted to.

She is the heart of your treasure now, and the dragon will never let her go."

At the word *dragon*, Rave felt Piper's struggles cease, and he could almost picture her ears pricking through her thick, black hair. A flash of Bale's teeth pierced the shadows in a Cheshire smile, and Rave wanted to curse his wicked king. Almost as badly as he wanted to cure his teasing brother.

He let out a jagged breath. "I thought I could finally return us to the way we were, before the petralys."

"There is no way back," Bale said. "The wind behind you is useless." He quoted the dragonkin wisdom with a twist of bitterness; he must know as well as Rave that no wind would carry him now.

"It's not over," Rave vowed.

But Bale only shook his head. "It might be. For you. I think your mate is none too pleased with you. You'd best consider what you will sacrifice to earn her forgiveness. Now go. I'm tired."

Rave tugged Piper backward.

She dug her heels in. "Dragon?"

Bale dragged in a rasping breath. And then blew out.

The candle exploded into a fireball that pushed back the darkness on all sides.

Pushed back Rave too, though his flesh was naturally resistant to fire. He yanked Piper behind him with an oath even as the fireball instantly collapsed upon itself.

If his brother crisped one hair on her dark head...

He hoped he'd pulled her away quickly enough to

block the view of the room exposed by the overzealous flame.

The stalactites dripping from the ceilings, almost meeting the stalagmites below, likes rows of serrated teeth, were disturbing enough. But the sight of Bale emblazoned on his dazzled eyeballs...

"Ask your mate," Bale rumbled.

Fuck.

Rave bumped Piper toward the elevator shaft, using his whole body to shield her. And to prevent her from whisking around him.

"What was...?" she sputtered, tugging ineffectually at Rave's outspread arm.

The damned elevator couldn't come fast enough. He cursed out a relieved oath when the door opened, letting out its square of innocuous electric light.

"Wait." Bale's growl was a king's command, forcing Rave to a halt.

At least Piper swallowed the rest of her question.

"On your hand," Bale said. The words rolled deep in his throat, like thunder after the flash of lightning. Warning of a deadly storm to come. "What is that?"

Rave looked down at Piper's grasp on his bicep. On her little finger was a silver and gold ring with an obsidian cabochon, in materials and workmanship nearly identical to the one he'd seen on her before. This was a new addition to her hands, and it didn't seem right to him. The warm glow of the copper-flecked sunstone better reflected her spirit.

Rave gave Piper a little squeeze, wordlessly urging

her to answer. Not that he thought Bale would hurt them. But he heard the dragon on edge.

Piper cleared her throat. "It's my friend's ring. Anjali made it for Esme. But she left it behind. I found it on her nightstand when I went to look for them." She twisted the braided metal around her finger. "It's silly, but I wanted to keep it close."

"Leave it here," Bale said.

Piper's head snapped up. And once again, Rave was stunned by her boldness.

"No," she said. "I'll give it to Ez when she comes back."

To Rave's continuing surprise, Bale gentled his tone. "You will do that," he agreed. "But in the meantime, there's something about it... I might be able to gather some insights into her whereabouts."

Piper shot a glance at Rave.

He nodded at her. "Bale knows things sometimes."

"Knows things," she repeated skeptically.

He gave her a small shrug. "I think it's weird too."

After a long moment, she spun the ring off her finger. She looked at it then let out a sharp breath.

"Leave it there on the floor," Bale said. "I'll summon you, brother, if anything comes to me. Otherwise, don't return."

Some of Piper's audacity must've rubbed off on him, because Rave wanted nothing more than to flip off his liege. Instead, he inclined his head and stepped back into the elevator.

Piper set the ring down, hesitated just a second,

then joined him.

He pressed the down button as soon as the curve of her ass cleared the doorway.

"What—?"

He squeezed her hand to silence her.

They rode down without a word.

He'd been too keen on getting her away to pay attention to what button he pushed, but as the silence stretched on, he realized he was taking them to the very bottom.

To the garden.

When the door chimed and let them out, he led her down the short passage through the silver gate to the center of the garden.

The waterfall was off, and the pool was a silvery mirror reflecting the daylight far above. Fern fronds around the water and the leaves of the climbing vines danced gently in some faint breeze only they could feel.

He could, however, feel the laser-focused intensity of Piper's glare between his shoulder blades. He'd have to jump in the pool to put out the flames.

He spun slowly on his boot heel to face her. Time to pay his Piper.

She had her arms crossed over her chest, fingers drumming in rhythmless agitation on her biceps. The remaining sunstone ring glinted on her finger.

"You told me not to be scared of your brother. But you didn't say he was..." She flapped one hand.

"The transformation you saw is because of the petralys." He circled around her to sit beside the pool, hoping she'd join him.

Instead, she paced a short distance away. "I've documented significant physical deviation in response to absorbed environmental contaminants, but that... Is that going to happen to you?"

He wasn't going to tell her he could shift to dragon any time. That wasn't what she was asking, anyway. Bale's situation was not the same. "It would have," he said. "But you stopped it."

"Because I'm your solarys."

That wasn't a question either, but he nodded. "I've never really believed in soul mates," he confessed.

She stopped her erratic pacing and spun to face him. "You don't?"

He grimaced. "It sounds too fantastical, doesn't it?"

"Compared to...?" She steepled her fingers against her forehead and peered at him suspiciously through the cage of her own hand. "I thought you'd try to convince me."

He'd thought so too. But she didn't want to believe, and he wasn't going to force her.

At that decision, the tension within him loosened. The dragon surrendering? That would only let the blight progress more quickly, but better to turn to stone than have her come to hate him for ruining the life she'd worked so hard to create for herself. That was her treasure, and he would not steal it from her.

"I wanted to find a cure," he said. "It was wrong of me to think of you as only that, a substance that fulfilled a need of mine." He gave her a crooked grin. "You are more than that, obviously."

She snorted. "A pain in that ass, or so I've heard."

"Bale has been out of circulation for awhile. He's forgotten his manners."

"Plus, he's a king." She watched him closely, watching for his reaction.

He didn't give her one, returning her gaze blandly.

If she didn't want to be part of his world, then he had to keep some secrets. The ones that could hurt her or scare her.

Or the ones that would scar him forever. Like admitting he *wanted* her to stay.

Her solarys power had freed the dragon within him, but for her own good, he would lock it back in its chains.

At least until she was gone.

He wondered how long he had until the petralys crept back.

"My brother can be an ass too," he acknowledged. "But it's good to have his assistance tracking your friends."

She snorted. "Like he's a psychic?"

"Eh, more like a bloodhound." Once upon a time, Bale Dorado had lit up the sky with his fire and the brilliance of his wings. Now he couldn't leave his cold, dark cave. But his dragonkin affinity for hunting down precious metals and stones might give them a clue to the whereabouts of Esme Montenegro and Anjali Herne with their bespelled rings.

Rave trailed his fingers in the pool, watching the

ripples spread.

With a sigh softer than the touch of water on his skin, Piper sank to the ledge seat beside him. "I'm sorry I couldn't help him."

"That's not on you. It's on me." Maybe if his dragon hadn't claimed her first... But no, Bale knew more than anyone about solarys; if he said a dragon chose only one heart for its treasure, then it was so. "I'll stay on it. And really, the prospect of searching for your friends seemed to bring back some of his, uh, energy."

He slanted a glance at her to see her frowning thoughtfully at the ripples.

She didn't look at him when she said, "I think we should call off the search."

He stiffened. "Why?"

"Because I think I was wrong. I couldn't understand why Esme agreed to marry Lars Ashcraft, when he seemed like just some rich, aloof, controlling jerk. But I..." Her gaze darted to him then away again. "I get it now. Even if I didn't, it's not for me to say. Anj tried to tell me that, but I didn't want to listen. That's why they left: because of me."

Rave took her hand, forcing her attention to him. Her fist tightened in his, the sunstone in her ring nestled in his palm. "You might have been influenced by your feelings, but that doesn't mean you were wrong. The staff hired to be your entourage is off the grid, and your friend Anjali somehow tampered with our security system. You thought something was going on, and you *weren't* wrong. As soon as Torch or Bale have a lead, I'll be there."

When she only stared at him miserably, he feathered his other hand through her hair. "You have a pure, innocent heart, Piper Ramirez. I am honored to have a place beside you, just for this little while."

He leaned forward to kiss the crown of her head, inhaling her cinnamon honey essence for what he knew must soon be the last time.

She eased her hand up his chest, flattening over his left pec, and tilted her head back.

It seemed as natural as striking flint to steel, to brush his mouth over hers, capturing her slow breath. Her lips parted, her tongue licking out like the first flame from a smoldering ember.

From there, the conflagration was inevitable and unstoppable.

Their clothes disappeared like smoke shredded by the wind, and all her gloriously dusky skin was revealed to his ravenous gaze. And hands. She was silk and heat and undulating curves of want that fired his own desires.

He laid her down in the soft moss of the grotto hidden behind the waterfall. But when she rolled to put him underneath her, he went more than willingly.

She straddled him, her breasts hanging ripe and lovely above him. He took one lush globe in his hand and tongued her nipple to a long, stiff peak. Her clit pouted almost as hard when he found the nub with his gently circling thumb. She rode his hand to a silent, shuddering climax, her head thrown back, eyes closed.

He thought maybe she was done with him already,

but when she opened her eyes, glazed darkly with pleasure, he caught a glimpse of the fire burning deeper in her.

She took his rampant cock in his hand and tilted the turgid flesh toward her well-slicked pussy.

"Piper," he murmured.

"I have an IUD, and I'm clean. And I trust you're safe too, right?"

He wasn't, not at all, but not for the reasons she meant right now. He nodded rigidly and groaned as she lowered herself slowly, taking inch after inch of his aching cock into her honeyed depths. The ancient rhythm she beat on his flesh had his heart pounding in answer.

But he clamped his jaw shut to hold back any awkward words.

When she came again in a violent rush, he flipped her across the moss. The crushed green smell and the musky sweetness of her satisfaction swirled in his head, soothing the inferno of his need.

For a few moments. He stoked her again, higher this time, until she wrapped her heels behind his ass and drew him all the way in. He cupped one hand behind her neck, forcing her to look up at him, to meet his gaze, to see...

No, she couldn't see what he was.

"Rave," she gasped. "Again."

He thrust into her again and again until she was keening, the sweet sound echoing off the rocks and reverberating in his bones.

She bowed up, slamming her pussy around his cock, and came with a hoarse scream.

His roar matched hers, his dragon claiming her as the heart of his treasure.

CHAPTER THIRTEEN

Reclining back in the warm, still pool, her head cushioned on Rave's pec, Piper stared up at the late-winter sky high above the garden.

Everything was topsy-turvy here: a garden at the bottom of a deep well, and a cave in the penthouse of a skyscraper. Friends who left her, and a stranger who would let his brother die rather than demand her blood. Her determination at the beginning of this trip to fight for old dreams replaced by a tentative reach for impossible realities.

No wonder she was so confused.

She rolled to her side to sling her arm across Rave's chest, sloshing blood-warm water across his tattoos, making them glimmer with life.

Just beyond the tip of her nose was the empty spot above his heart.

Bale had told Rave that *she* was the heart of his treasure. What did that even mean? She traced her finger over the hollow space.

Rave caught her hand and lifted it to his lips. "Piper." His breath gusted hot across her pulse point.

His phone rang, and he let out a curse.

Their clothes were scattered on the far end of the pool, and he splashed hurriedly through the water to get to his jeans. She bit her lip to hold back a smile at the hint of a jiggle in his taut ass.

But as the call started to go to voice mail and she heard Torch's first words—"We found them"—her smile cut out.

She scrambled across the pool with far more jiggling than Rave.

He was already talking to his cousin by the time she joined him. He held up one finger when she gestured for him to switch to speaker.

"All right," he said while she jittered impatiently. "I'm on my way... No. Don't make a move until I get there."

Piper scrambled to pull on her clothes over her wet skin. "No what? Where are they? Where are we going?"

"No, meaning you aren't going anywhere." He clamped his hand on her shoulder, trapping her with only one arm through her sleeve.

She scowled at him. "Of course I'm going."

"You aren't. Because I'm not taking you, and I'm not telling you where they are."

She sagged a little under the weight of his hand. "You're being overbearing."

But the hard set of his jaw told her he wasn't budging.

"Torch said it's possible Esme may have been trying to leave Ashcraft. And that Anjali may have stopped her."

Piper wavered on her feet. "But... Ez was mad at me when I..." She thought back. It had actually been Anjali mad at her, mostly. But Anj didn't like Lars any more than she did.

Or hadn't.

When she stopped struggling, Rave lifted his hand so she could finish dressing. He donned his clothing easily, and it seemed as if all the water had steamed off his hot body.

He watched while she tugged on her shoes. "When you said Ashcraft is rich and controlling, did you mean dangerous?"

Piper stiffened. "You think he hurt Esme?"

"Don't know. But that's why you aren't going. I'm not risking you."

"Lars wouldn't..." She put her hand over her mouth and realized she couldn't say something she wasn't sure she believed. Slowly she lowered her hand. "He might. He's always gotten what he wanted. He wants Esme, always has."

"Then maybe it's time we see what Esme wants." Rave gripped her nape, holding her fast as he stared at her hard. "You trusted me with your body, with your pleasure. Will you trust me to bring your friends back? Will you stay here while I do that?"

She curled her lips between her teeth and finally nodded, as much as she could considering his remorseless grasp.

"Good." He leaned down and kissed her, one fierce, hot slant of his mouth across hers, then he released her. "I'll be back. Wait for me."

He turned and strode away, already talking on his phone again.

She sagged, bracing herself on the pool ledge behind her. Esme had tried to run away? Anjali had kidnapped her? But Lars had people—spies or jailers?—surrounding them. Where were they? None of it made sense.

And she was waiting around some grotto pool like a helpless princess.

That made even less sense when she'd always been the helpful, hardworking one. Princesses didn't have calluses.

Worse, she didn't have her cell phone. And secret gardens probably didn't have landlines. What if Esme had been trying to call her? Or Anj?

What if Rave needed her?

Before the thought ended, she was heading for the elevator—and she couldn't even believe she'd taken those ass-master marble stairs when there'd be an elevator—but as soon as she got her phone, she'd come right back in case Rave returned here.

As she hopped into the elevator though, she realized the buttons didn't stop for every floor. Well, of course it wouldn't since this was a private lift. But at least she'd get closer to the main floor—

The door closed and she found herself heading up before she'd selected any of the buttons.

Oo-kay.

She was only half surprised when the door opened into blackness.

This time she kept one foot firmly in the doorway; damned elevator wasn't going anywhere without her.

"How'd you know it was me?" she asked the shadows.

"My brother and cousin are away. And of those remaining who know of this path, only you would dare use it."

"Easier than the stairs," she grumbled.

Bale rumbled; his version of laughter, she'd guessed.

"Why'd you summon me?" That was the word he'd used with Rave, though it sounded old-fashioned to her ear. But probably kings preferred old fashions.

"I have no doubt Rave told you to stay put, and yet you were roaming the Keep. Why?"

"I needed my phone," she said. Then she admitted, "And I don't like being told what I can't do." If she'd let that happen, she'd have dropped out of college. Hell, she never would've made it to college, never met Esme and Anjali. Never set foot in the Keep.

"That will be good for my brother. He can be imperious at times."

She choked on her own laugh.

"You're thinking we're much alike." His voice was wry.

She inclined her head. "I wouldn't disagree with a king."

"In that case, you'll agree when I tell you to go after him."

She stiffened in the doorway. "Go after Rave? But why? Torch said he found Esme. They're going to get her and come right back."

"It's not going to be that simple."

She took a jolting step out of the elevator, her heartbeat racing ahead of her. "Why not? What's happening?"

"The ring you gave me. Esme's ring." The rasping voice dropped an octave in a way that sent a shiver down Piper's spine. "There was magic on it. Alchemical magic."

Piper shook her head hard. "I—I'm sorry. What?"

"I've been told you are a chemical engineer. Surely you've heard of the alchemists."

Not in her chemistry classes. She had to dredge up memories of her undergraduate English requirement. "They weren't chemists. They were wannabes, always trying to turn lead into gold."

"Close. They were always trying to turn *everything* into gold. And they weren't wannabes. They were warlocks."

Piper groped for the frame of the doorway, for support or for escape she wasn't sure. But somehow she'd gotten too far away from it. "Warlocks. Uh-huh."

Had the petralys broken his mind?

Wait a second. She was willing to believe in a rare blood-born contaminant that turned men into stone and another *more* uncommon substance that turned their blood back into rainbows, but she was going to quibble over the word *magic*?

In her consternation, she hardly noticed when the elevator door closed, shutting her in with the disfigured lunatic.

"Are you one of them?" Red eyes gleamed in the

darkness, closer than she expected.

She staggered back another step. Her heel caught on something, and she went down hard, knocking her elbow on the concrete with a sharp twinge that sent tears rushing into her eyes. "I'm not a warlock."

"You'd be a witch, actually."

"What? I'm not!"

"Hold out your hand."

Baffled, she did so. Although what it would prove to him—

The sunstone in her ring glowed, brightening the space around her, shining on the slick rock of the stalagmite that had tripped her.

A darker shadow twisted just beyond the reach of her ring. Something metallic rasped on the stone floor. Bale, pacing.

"So. Not a witch?"

"It's never done that," she whispered. "I've had it forever, ever since..."

"Ever since your friend Anjali made it for you. As she made Esme the obsidian ring."

Piper nodded jerkily. "What did you find in Esme's ring?"

"Darkness. Death."

She stared in horror at her own ring, then frantically tried to twist it off. Her fingers scrabbling at it cast bars of shadows across the room.

"Stop it." Impatience roughened Bale's voice. "I don't sense any of that from the sunstone. Yours has only light, warmth." He hesitated. "And love."

His longing resonated in her, but she pushed it away, needing to focus. "Then why—?"

"Something changed. Changed the stone. Changed your friend. I'm not sure which. And my brother will be in the thick of it."

She scrambled to her feet. "You have to warn him."

"I will. And you have to go to him. I fear he will need his true mate before the night is done."

CHAPTER FOURTEEN

The motel—accurately called "Mot-l" according to the broken sign—on the outskirts of town was as dark and quiet as the Strip was neon and gleeful chaos. The mottled stucco building seemed to squat beneath its two-stories of outside-access rooms, and the ubiquitous palm trees planted in the gravel beside the cracked asphalt of the parking lot all leaned away as if longing to escape.

Rave didn't blame them.

"Of course she'd go dark," Torch said, anticipation clipping the ends of his words. "Just like she did at the Keep. When Bale called with the vision he got through the ring, I instantly thought of this place."

"How convenient you know all the worst dives," Rave said dryly.

"Hey, sometimes you need to go somewhere no one asks questions."

Rave didn't want to know what those times were. Or what the questions might be. "You're certain Piper's friends are here?"

"Showed the desk clerk a picture from our security tape. For a mere twenty bucks, he confirmed they are both in room seven, bottom floor at the end." Torch cracked his knuckles. "Couldn't've made themselves easier to snatch if they tried."

Rave sat back in the passenger seat of the gray work SUV. He'd never even seen this vehicle at the Keep. If he had, he would've asked Torch to keep an eye on it since it looked sketchy, but in the Mot-l parking lot, it blended right in.

"I assume we're just busting in the door," he said.

Torch gave him serious side eye. "Nooo," he drawled. "That would be tacky. We're going to wait until they order takeout and are all distracted by yummy fried things or pepperoni things. *Then* we are going to bust in the door."

"I assume you'll confiscate their takeout."

"Wouldn't want to leave evidence."

They observed the room in silence a moment.

"Why did they come to the Keep at all, if they were just going to relocate here?" Rave mused.

Torch shrugged. "Bad taste. Ran out of money. Whatever. We can ask her all the questions we want once we have her." He smacked his lips as if he already had the Chinese food *and* pizza *and* the females in his grasp.

Rave frowned at his cousin. Torch strutted in his black leather like there wasn't anything else underneath—probably there wasn't—but he *did* have a brain. It wasn't like him not to be focused on the *why* along with all the other Ws when it came to the Keep's security and the secrets of the Nox Incendi.

But he seemed fixated on Anjali.

Maybe because she was the only one who'd ever gotten away.

Rave knew how that felt.

"Piper is a solarys," he said.

"Uh huh." Torch leaned forward to rest his chin on the backs of his hands folded over the steering wheel, staring at room seven. If he'd had a tail in this form, it would be lashing impatiently.

"But she didn't affect Bale."

That brought Torch's attention around. "When did she see him?"

"I took her to his lair."

Torch winced. "Dude."

"She didn't see anything." Rave hesitated. "Nothing she would believe. I hoped her presence would reverse his petralys."

With a shake of his head, Torch said, "She's *your* true mate. Not his."

Rave's dragon screamed a silent agreement. But Rave knew better than the beast: she wasn't his either. She couldn't be, not when he'd spent centuries seeking a cure.

"I can't keep her," he said.

His cousin stilled, eyes narrowing. "She is the heart of your treasure. Without her, you'll never be complete."

"There has to be another way to save Bale."

"We aren't talking about him now. We're talking about you."

"Bale is our liege."

"You're of the same blood. And for a long time now, the fire of the Nox Incendi has burned higher in you. You've been in charge of the Keep. The kin would follow you—"

Rave slammed his fist up into the ceiling of the SUV. The metal dented with an almost draconic scream. "That is treason."

Torch merely looked at him, though lightning flickered dangerously in the back of his eyes. "When your brother made me head of security, it wasn't just for the Keep, but for the tribe. I will protect us. Even from your misplaced martyrdom."

Was he playing the martyr? Rave ignored the gleam of ichor across his torn knuckles. The opalescent sheen had returned, but only because of Piper. For the good of the tribe, could he afford to set her free?

Or would he lock her away and tell himself he had no choice?

"She didn't ask for this," he murmured.

Torch snorted. "Neither did you. But whatever. It's just a chance to save yourself and lead your dying people into a new era of hope. By all means, whine about it if it makes you feel better." He propped his chin on the steering wheel again, grumbling, "You won't catch *me* hesitating when I find *my* mate."

Rave wanted to punch *him* this time. Which only made it likely that his cousin was right.

He had to keep Piper, for his own sake and all the Nox Incendi. She seemed to like his grotto, and she'd said she liked working outside with her father, so maybe she could return the garden to its glory.

She wouldn't have anything else to do once he took her.

As the crown jewel of his hoard, she would have the finest clothes and most decadent jewels, the rarest wines and richest feasts. Everything but her freedom, since a dragon's hoard was always hidden away.

Piper would hate it. She would hate him.

Was it worth it, to be king?

As if he'd conjured a mirage out of his own desperate longing, a flash of movement in the side mirror caught his eye.

He cursed and thrust open the door.

"Piper," he hissed.

Behind him, Torch said something worse, but Rave was focused on his solarys, his true mate, the heart of his treasure.

The pain in his ass.

Her eyes widened as he strode toward her. She'd put on a black sweater over her clothes and pulled the hood over the loose coils of her dark hair—a concession to the secrecy and danger of the situation, he supposed.

Not that it made much difference; he swore he could sense every precious curve of her through the cloth.

His hands twitched as he grabbed her and hustled her into the back of the SUV.

"What are you doing here?" Rave snapped, echoing the words over Torch's identical question.

She glanced between them. "Bale didn't call?"

"No—" Rave's angry denial was cut short by the ring of Torch's cell phone.

As his cousin answered with the semi-deferential voice he only used with his liege, Rave tightened his grip on Piper. He'd yanked the SUV door closed behind her, so she had nowhere to go, and still he couldn't force his fingers apart.

Despite his grasp, which he knew was too tight, Piper's deep brown gaze was steady. "Your brother said you'd need me."

"I don't," Rave growled.

A lie, but not for the reasons under discussion.

A flash of hurt shadowed her eyes, but she only shrugged back her hood and lowered the sweater zipper with a sigh. "I wasn't going to say no to your brother."

Rave realized his attention was following the zipper and yanked his glare back to her. "How convenient."

To his shock, she gave him a little grin, "I know, right?" She finally squirmed against his hold. "Where are they? Esme and Anjali. They're here? Have you talked to them?"

"Not yet." Rave glanced over when Torch ended the call. His cousin answered his unspoken question with a shrug and a furrowed brow: he didn't know why Bale had sent Piper and he hadn't argued either. Rave wanted to roar at them both. But not where Piper would hear. "We're waiting."

She wrinkled her nose. "For what?"

"A strategic moment," Torch said in an eager tone that some might use to say "sweet and sour sauce".

Piper's wrinkled nose screwed up into a frown. "You think you're going in guns blazing?"

Torch grinned. "Not guns, no." He shot a sly glance at Rave.

Before that line of discussion went too far, Rave explained, "Torch has his people surrounding the motel. We were just waiting for a little distraction to keep your friends occupied while we moved in."

"Well, I'm here," Piper said. "I'll be your distraction."

"Perfect," Torch said, just as Rave said, "No."

When Torch and Piper gave him matching scowls, Rave shook his head. "You aren't going in there, Piper. There's more to this than you—"

"Magic," she interrupted. When he only gaped at her, she continued, "Bale explained. There's some sort of...alchemical magic being used against Esme and Anjali. I knew they were in trouble, but this..." She let out a huff of breath.

Rave's thoughts flapped like helpless hatchlings. How much and what exactly had Bale told her? He speared a glance at his cousin, but Torch shrugged.

If he was going to keep her, it didn't matter what she knew or didn't. She'd be his sacrifice, and that was that. But if he still believed he should let her go...

She put her hand over his. "Rave, let me help. They are my friends, and you're doing this for me, because of me. I don't know what they did to your cameras"—she tilted her head to include Torch in the conversation—"or why they ran away, but I want answers too."

She was right, and it wasn't like he really had a choice if Bale had sent her, but it was the touch that doomed him. If there was going to be any chance he could not just *take* her but *win* her, this was where it started.

He rammed open the SUV door. Probably with unnecessary force, judging from the way her dark eyes snapped wide, but he was trying.

"Go on," he said. "Room seven. We're right here. If you need me, call."

She reached for her phone. "I don't have your—"

"Not with that." He grasped her chin and lifted her gaze from the little screen to him. The blackest centers in her dark irises expanded, like a night sky where he could fall forever. Or fly. "Call to me."

Her tongue darted out to dampen her lips. "Call? To you?"

"Magic." He gave her a crooked smile. "Since you're an expert now."

Those dark eyes slanted half shut. "I'll find out what's going on."

He knew she didn't just mean with her friends. "Hopefully."

He sent her out into the emptiness across the parking lot.

Torch cleared his throat. "Magic? Really?"

"If she gets in any trouble, needs me in any way, I'll know." Rave watched as she whisked past the palm trees, feeling as if she was tearing a piece of him away as she went. "Anywhere she goes, whatever she wants, I'll know, like I know myself. She is my center now. My heart."

Torch dragged one hand down his jaw. "Uh. That seems a little...intense."

Rave smirked at him. "Good thing you won't hesitate

when you find yours."

Piper was achingly aware of Rave behind her.

His touch. His words. His...magic?

What had she gotten herself into?

But ahead of her was room seven and the friends who'd gotten her this far. She wasn't giving up on them just because she was a little confused.

Maybe one night in the Keep had spoiled her, but she couldn't believe Esme and Anj had picked this dump. Dead leaves had swirled up into the corner of the doorway, as if no one had passed that threshold in a very long time.

She swallowed against the bone-dryness in her throat and knocked softly. "Anj? Ez? It's Piper. Open up. Please?"

For a long moment, she thought no one would answer. Maybe this wasn't the right—

The door cracked open, and Anjali peered out, her red dreads leached of color by the crappy fluorescent light overhead. "What are you doing here?"

If anyone else asked her that tonight, Piper decided she was going to get a complex. "What are *you* doing here?" she countered. "This place is a pit."

"Easier to get out of a pit than a keep," Anj muttered. She grabbed Piper's hand and yanked her inside. "Did anybody see you?"

Piper stumbled behind her friend. As the door clicked shut and locked behind her, she almost wanted to call to Rave. But how did that work exactly?

She clamped down on her nerves. She'd volunteered for this. "Anj, what are you guys doing here?" She glanced around at the little room with its double beds and ugly bedspreads. Esme was lying on the far bed, curled on her side, seemingly asleep, her pinched face almost as pale as the over-bleached pillow case. She looked less like an enchanted princess and more like a corpse; the thought made Piper shiver.

"Why did you leave?" She couldn't keep the plaintive note out of the question.

And to her surprise, Anjali's gaze dropped, as if she actually felt bad. "I'm sorry. This wasn't supposed to include you. But I had to get away when you kept trying to get Ez to leave." She paced the worn carpet at the foot of the beds. "Nothing's going according to plan."

Piper edged around her pacing friend and settled on the corner of the far bed. She touched Esme's hand. The pale skin above the big diamond ring was icy cold. "What plan? The bachelorette party?"

She tried to keep her voice innocent, but Anj whirled, her flowing gypsy skirt a split second behind.

She stalked closer, eyes narrowing. "How did you find us, anyway?"

So much for innocent. Piper scrambled to come up with an answer that would convince Anjali she didn't know anything. But maybe she was done being the little sister of their trio.

She met her friend's suspicious gaze with a hard look of her own and said, "Magic."

If she'd half hoped Anj would laugh in her mocking way, she was sadly disappointed.

Instead, Anjali sank down onto the corner of her own bed. Her dusky complexion looked gray. "I always knew you were the smart little scientist. But I thought that meant you'd never question... When did you figure it out?"

Uh, about two seconds ago? Piper clenched her fists against the urge to grab Anjali and shake her, demand that she admit this was all an elaborate ruse, a bachelorette party trick.

She countered with a question of her own. "Why are you doing this?"

"Ashcraft." Anj let the word fall between them like a chunk of lead. "He said he'd let Ez go in exchange for Dorado blood."

Piper shook her head. Dammit, she'd found her friends, but now she had *more* questions, not fewer. "Why does Lars want the ichor? It's poisoned."

Except for Rave's. Because of her.

"Poisoned?" This time Anjali looked confused. "How do you know?"

Piper twisted her lips. "Science," she said wryly. "A disorder called petralys is contaminating the ichor, rendering it inert, useless."

Anj laughed, not a happy sound, more like a gurgle wrenched from her gut. "Good. We'll get Ez back, but the ash-hole won't get shit in return." Her laughter died, as did the momentary spark of vindictiveness in her eyes. "But he's too powerful already. What if he thinks we spiked the ichor to kill him?"

Piper's head ached trying to keep up with this mystery she barely understood. "Why does he want the ichor?"

"Why does everyone? Ashcraft is rich and powerful and ruthless as fuck, but he'd be a god among men if he captured a dragon's essence too."

With a blink, Piper scooted back, bumping her butt on Esme's bent knees. Ez let out a low moan, but her eyes remained tight clenched. "I... What?"

Bale had mentioned dragons before blowing out the candle in a fireball. Rave had shielded her and dragged her away, but not before she'd seen the bizarre cavern.

The stalagmites and stalactites had glittered, as if inlaid with gems.

And Rave had refused to answer her when she asked about...

Dragons.

She couldn't believe it. Bale was a dragon.

And Rave was a dragon's blood brother.

Which meant Rave was a...dragon.

Luckily for her, Anjali seemed as stunned and uncertain as she felt. "We can't give Ashcraft the poisoned ichor until he frees Esme. He has alchemically bound her to him, to control her. If he dies while she's under his spell, she'll die too."

Dragons. Spells. Death. It was too much. Piper bit her lip.

Anjali reached across the gap between the beds to take her hand. "I should've told you. I didn't want you involved, didn't want anyone else getting hurt, but I should've known you'd help. You were always the one holding us together."

Piper stared at her friend. Holding them together? Did they really see her that way? She thought she'd always been the one tagging along.

A shock quivered through her as the sunstone in her ring brightened, gold as a flame. Anjali's fire opal flared in answer. In Piper's other hand, Esme's fingers tightened.

Anj smiled, a little misty eyed. "See? I didn't understand it when I made the rings—shit, I wouldn't have believed any of this at the time—but I always knew there was power in our friendship. It's always been the three of us." Her grip tightened. "But there's more to magic than sparkles, Pipsqueak. We're in trouble." The sheen of tears darkened her hazel eyes, like oil on the bayou of her childhood home. "Black magic trouble."

"And of course I want to help," Piper said, pulling away from both her friends. "But we can't just take the ichor. It's what keeps them...the dragons alive."

"All the more reason to take it." Anj spat melodramatically to one side. "One monster's blood can kill another monster."

"They aren't monsters," Piper protested. Well, maybe Bale was... "And if they were, they wouldn't meekly lie down and give up their essence just for a pretty-please."

"No. That's unicorns." Anj waved her ringed hand impatiently. "But dragons are just as surely drawn to virgins as sacrifice." Her mouth turned grim. "The only thing Ashcraft didn't take from Esme."

Piper tried not to gape. Esme was a virgin? When they'd lived together, Anj had crowed about her conquests, Piper had blushed about hers, and—now that she thought about it—Esme had always been coy and giggly. But...never?

"She was probably the only virgin in the Keep," Piper muttered.

"That was the plan," Anjali said. "If we put her out there, one of the dragons would come for her." She looked at their willowy blond friend curled helplessly on the bed, and her mouth turned down another degree. "Who could resist?"

Piper stared at her friend. She'd always thought Anjali Herne was the supremely confident, almost arrogant, one of their trio. To find out Anj too had doubts made Piper wonder how much of her own insecurity was self-inflicted.

But she didn't have time to diagnose her own limitations. "Anj, this is wrong. We can't take the dragons' ichor. We can't use Ez as bait. I know Lars is an ash-hole—"

"You have no idea," Anjali said.

"But whatever makes him think he can do this is just plain wrong. And we won't let him win.'"

To her horror, Anjali's sloe eyes quickened with tears. "Pipsqueak, you are too good for this world. I knew the sunstone was perfect for you; your spirit is fiery bright. But we can't fight Ashcraft." Her breath caught. "We can't."

Piper hadn't seen her friend so beaten since she'd had to quit school to work at her uncle's head shop. And now that it turned out magic was real, and somehow Anj was part of it, Piper had to wonder what else went on in that funky place with its even funkier smells. "What happened, Anj? What did Lars tell you to make you do this?"

Anjali's jaw hardened. "It doesn't matter. The dragons are evil and don't belong here. Sacrificing one to get Esme away is just a bonus. And if the contaminated ichor kills Ashcraft, let's get this party started."

This wasn't a bachelorette party anymore; it was a nightmare. Piper didn't want to imagine what the hangover was going to be like. "Maybe we can't fight Lars, but the dragons can. I know they would."

Anj shook her head, her dreadlocks lashing with her agitation. "Why would they? They don't care about humans. We're just a source of blood and treasure to them."

Piper bit her lips. Was that true? She couldn't figure out what Rave saw in her. Besides the solarys power. "I'm pretty sure they'd care about a human sneaking around hoping to steal their ichor." She tucked her hands under her thighs. "I could call one and ask."

Anjali stiffened. "Call one? What, like you have a dragon on speed dial?"

"Not exactly." Piper squirmed uncomfortably on the scratchy bedspread. "That's how I found you. One of them told me you were here. And there are couple, maybe more, out there now."

Springing like a jack-in-the-box to her feet, Anj raced the few steps to the door. Then she just stared at it. "Oh fuck. Like one deadbolt is going to keep them out." She whirled to face Piper. "Are you insane? I took Ez away from the Keep because I thought you were going to get us in trouble with Ashcraft, trying to convince her to leave him. But you brought dragons down on our heads instead?"

"I didn't bring them," Piper corrected. "They found you and told me. They were helping me, and I think they'd help again if I told them what's happening to Esme." She wasn't so sure what was happening with Anj, but one problem at a time.

Her friend paced, skirt kicking up with every step. "I can still make this work," she mumbled. "If there's a dragon already here..." She spun toward her oversized purse and rifled through it.

As her muttering got louder and less sensible, Piper pushed slowly off the bed. She edged toward the door.

She still didn't understand everything that was going on, but it was enough to know Ez was in trouble, and Anj too, and Lars and magic were at the root of it, and Rave and the dragons—dragons!—were the targets, and *she* was going to stop it and get her answers. In water purification, powerful UV light—like the purest, most concentrated sunlight—was used to kill off germs, and it was time to throw open the curtains on this mysterious place. Or, since they were in Vegas, it was time to put all the cards on the table.

When she clicked back the deadbolt, Anjali spun around. "What are you doing? Don't go out there yet. I have to set the snare."

"No." Piper spun the doorknob and pulled, letting in the whiff of cold desert night. "No more secrets."

Anj lunged for her, stiff-arming the door. It slammed shut. "Okay, okay. I'll explain everything. But the snare will protect us. Just let me—"

The door blew open.

Not with a chilly breeze, but with the roar of a blast furnace.

CHAPTER FIFTEEN

The dragon was too close under his skin, and Rave couldn't hold back its hoarse cry and the heat of its anger when he knocked on—okay, smashed—the door of room seven.

He'd sensed Piper's worry and her confusion. And worse of all, her doubt.

She needed him, wanted him, but hadn't called out to him because she didn't believe in him.

The dragon wouldn't wait any longer.

He managed to keep it contained in the boundaries of his human shape, unleashing its fury only on the cheap plywood.

Piper had dodged back, but now she held out both hands, blocking him more effectively than the door. "No, Rave. Go back. It's not safe. There's a trap—"

Her red-headed troublemaking friend, Anjali, stepped out from behind her. There was something in her hand. A glass orb, black.

She threw the orb at him.

She was fast, but his reflexes were the dragon's and he dodged.

Torch bulled through the doorway behind him, his stare locked intently. Not on the threat. On Anjali.

Rave shoved him, but his cousin's tank-like build resisted the blow.

The orb struck Torch in the shoulder and shattered. Though the tinkling chime was a testament to the fragility of the thin-blown glass, the force contained within spun Torch a one-eighty, throwing him into the wall.

Rave had managed to push Torch almost out of the way; if the orb had struck him square in the chest...

Tendrils of oily black smoke sprang from the broken glass like tentacles from a rotting kraken. The stench was worse than that.

Torch coughed and swatted at the smoke, reaching through the haze toward Anjali. He bared his teeth in a vicious smile.

And the blackness sank into his skin.

His eyes widened, then rolled back in his head.

As he hit the floor, the crash was louder than the door going down.

Rave swung away from his cousin, but the tendrils that had missed Torch were questing outward, seeking prey.

And Piper was in the way.

He reached for her, dangerously close to the black smoke that had felled Torch, but she danced back.

"Get out, Rave," she gasped. "It's a dragon trap."

A cold shock nearly extinguished the dragon in him.

She knew. She knew what he was.

Had she known what her friends were doing?

He flinched away from the still-expanding tentacle. It struck with an almost sentient ferocity. He whirled in the tight confines of the tiny room, but the tendril sliced past his neck.

His skin exploded with pain that radiated up into his jaw and down his arm. The muscles there seized, and he clamped his other hand over the area.

Those fingers went numb.

The tentacle coiled back, darting down his leg. Pain, numbness. He fell to one knee.

'Rave!' Piper jolted around the end of the bed toward him, but her friend hauled her back.

"Don't touch him," Anjali hissed. "Not until the snare locks tight."

Piper tried to wrench away. "Stop it. Anj, he's here to help us!"

"He will help us. Well...his ichor will."

Rave tried to retort, but his jaw was frozen shut. He tried to draw in a breath, to ignite the dragon, but inside, all was darkness and stone. His lungs heaved to pull air past his closed throat.

Shadows threatened at the edges of his vision.

Anjali pulled a phone from her bag. To dial she had to release Piper who ran to his side.

She dropped to her knees in front of him. "Rave. Rave, what can I do?" Her hands hovered near him. "I'm your solarys. Maybe I can—"

He managed to throw himself backward to avoid her touch. He couldn't let the smoke get to her.

Her eyes widened. "Rave. I didn't know, I swear."

Anjali yanked her to her feet. "C'mon. They'll be here soon."

Piper resisted. "Who? The dragons?"

"Ashcraft's men. They'll deal with Dorado."

"Anj, no. You're wrong. We can't do this!"

"We have to. I have to." The red-head's eyes were wild with something like panic. "I already did."

Piper wrenched free and stood over him. "I won't let them steal his ichor."

Anjali went to the far bed and pulled the blonde upright. Esme Montenegro looked more like a sack of boiled potatoes than the elegant heiress he'd seen on the security cams.

Although he supposed he shouldn't talk.

Well, he couldn't anyway.

Anjali dragged the stumbling Esme toward the door, stomping over the unmoving Torch. Was he dead? He'd taken most of the hit from the black orb.

Piper blocked his view of his cousin when she knelt beside him again.

With the wall at his back, he couldn't move any farther away, and this time she put her hands on him.

She framed his face, straining his frozen muscles to lift his gaze to hers. "What do I do? How do I make the solarys thing work?"

With the shadows encroaching all around, she filled his vision. He couldn't form any words, just a low, draconic rumble.

Her hands tightened on his cheeks. "If you have to take my blood, my treasure, my life, whatever, do it. If Anjali is doing this for Lars Ashcraft, they are both wrong, and you have to stop them."

Though it took all the strength left in his numbed

arm, he raised his hand to cover hers. Through the chill of his skin, her fingers felt like brands, burning him.

Just the way he liked it.

"Piper," he whispered.

She gasped, and then she was being dragged away from him.

Two men in dark, unmarked clothing hauled her, kicking and shouting, toward the door. Another man—in Keep livery—was bending over Torch.

Rave recognized him from the security crew. What was his name? Antonio. A newer hire, but certainly vetted as all their employees were.

Torch was going to be livid.

If he lived.

Piper grabbed at the doorframe, but her fingers slipped off the splintered plywood, and she disappeared into the night. Her screams cut out abruptly.

Rave wrenched at the invisible bonds enchaining him.

Did one slip?

Had Piper's touch loosened the black tendrils creeping in his muscles?

One of the men returned and stood beside Antonio. "Did you get it?"

Antonio brandished an iron knife, like the one Rave used to excise the ichor running through his veins. "Give me a minute. The bitch over-delivered and now we have to bleed two of them."

The man slanted a nervous look at Rave. "One is fine. Let's just get out of here."

Antonio scoffed. "You think *he* will be understanding if we walk away without both? Yeah, I'll let him know that's what you decided and we'll see how that goes for you."

"Fine." The man stomped across the little room toward Rave. "I'll get this one then."

He pulled a skinning knife from his boot.

Maybe it was because Torch had taken the worst of the hit, or maybe it was Piper's touch, but before the knife cleared the leather, Rave lunged upright.

His leg was still weak and nearly buckled under his weight. But that just made his attack more unpredictable, and when the man swung at him with the wicked blade, Rave was already coming down on him like a fucking mountain slide.

His slashing hand broke the man's arm, sending the knife spinning across the room. The man's stunned shriek ended with Rave's hand around his throat.

He lifted Ashcraft's flunky off his boots and flung him at Antonio, knocking the security man off Torch.

Both humans went down in a tangle of flailing limbs.

But Rave's numb knee failed him and he stumbled into the bed. With a burst of frustration, he tried to shove himself upright. Despite the roar trapped in his chest, whatever energy had possessed him guttered out, and he sprawled across the corner, the bedspread slipping under his weight.

Antonio struggled upright, dislodging the other man.

At the sight of his prey escaping, Rave summoned up another surge of fury.

The two humans must have seen their death in his eyes. They scrambled for the doorway.

Antonio's knife was still wedged in Torch's neck.

The dull meteorite iron was one of the few substances that could damage Nox Incendi dragonhide, but it was a little overkill for their human shapes. Ignoring the agonizing prickle of nerves and muscles coming back to life, Rave dragged himself across the floor to his cousin.

Torch's eyes were open, and the dragon's vertical slit pupils glared at Rave above the bone hilt.

"This is going to sting," Rave warned him.

He yanked out the knife.

Not a sound from Torch. Blood spurted from the wound, and ichor welled behind it. Rave clamped his hand over the gash, giving the ichor a moment to stop the arterial spray.

But his whole body yearned for the open doorway. From his crouch, holding Torch's life in with his hand, Rave couldn't see the parking lot, but the screech of tires told him what he needed to know.

He felt his heart was being torn from his body as gruesomely as the knife flaying to bone.

But he couldn't leave his cousin to die, picked apart by those human vultures.

Viciously ignoring the ache of the black smoke in his body, Rave lifted Torch to his shoulder and staggered out to the battered SUV.

A dark form in Keep livery appeared from behind the vehicle. If he hadn't been weighed down by Torch, Rave might've punched first and asked questions later, but after a split second, he recognized Torch's second-in-command, another dragon-shifter.

"What the hell happened?" Lucius yanked open the door.

"Where the hell were you?" Rave shot back. The words were only partly garbled, his neck still aching from the touch of the alchemical magic.

"Torch said to hold back." Luc helped lay Torch in the rear of the SUV. "He said the females were probably being watched, tailed at least, and he wanted to draw out their accomplices."

Rave cursed over the sound of Torch's breathless groan. "So he wanted to use them as bait, but they were the bait for us. What a clusterfuck."

He fished the keys from Torch's pocket. "Let's go."

Luc slammed the door shut. "Where to?"

"To win back my solarys."

Piper huddled Esme against her shoulder and avoided looking across the limo at the man with the gun.

He was dressed in a uniform with the Keep logo on the breast patch of the shirt.

And there was blood on his hands.

At least a few drops of it was probably hers from where he'd cracked her across the mouth to stop her screams. Her lower lip was swollen and aching, and she guessed she'd find bruises on her shins. He'd pushed her into the limo, making her trip on the door frame. By the time she'd gotten herself upright, Esme was being dumped on top of her. And then the limo was screeching away.

Next to gun-guy sat another man, cradling his arm as carefully as Piper held Esme. His face was splotchy with sweat, and Piper thought she could probably take him. If she had Anjali at her back...

But her friend—was Anj still a friend when she was working with Ashcraft's goons?—slumped on the limo seat beside her, looking out the window.

Maybe she didn't want to see the gun either. But she'd been waiting quietly in the limo with Esme when gun-guy threw Piper inside. Obviously, Anjali had made her choice.

If ever there was a time to call out to Rave, this was it.

Piper cleared her throat. "Where are you taking us?"

"Shut up," gun-guy said, his tone casual and conversational though his words were not.

She'd never been good at confrontation and always kept her head down, so she had no idea what to do next. Did she need to know where she was for Rave to find her? Would he even come? Or did he think she'd been part of the conspiracy to steal a dragon's ichor?

To her surprise, Anjali straightened away from the window, reaching for her purse. "I'm going to call Ashcraft. I kept my end of the bargain, and you need to let us go."

"No." Gun-guy jittered the weapon in his hand, making Piper catch her breath at his carelessness. "Mr. Ashcraft is going to be furious that you lost the ichor. He doesn't need to hear about it any sooner than necessary."

Anjali's lip curled in a sneer. "I didn't lose it. I served those dragons to you on a fucking platter, and you couldn't even carve them up."

Gun-guy swore viciously. Piper had to agree; it hadn't been *quite* so easy as Anjali was making it sound.

Not that she was going to defend either of them to evil Lars.

But what *could* she do? There were the two men across from her and the driver, at least. Esme was defenseless and useless. Anjali seemed to have rolled her dice...and lost.

She'd have to take her own chance if she saw one.

But she didn't.

The road outside the limo was dark, but she recognized the straight line of lights when they finally slowed. The airfield.

Maybe once she would've been grateful to get out of Vegas considering she hadn't wanted to come in the first place. But now...

She'd be leaving Rave behind and heading into Ashcraft's clutches.

This had to be her chance—

Gun-guy grabbed Esme from her hold and hauled her out of the limo. Ez's cute heeled boots were dragged off her feet, and her stockinged heels bumped along the pavement. When Piper started to go after them, he paused and pointed the gun at her.

"Mr. Ashcraft doesn't need you."

Piper froze, staring down that black bore that was scarier than anything she'd seen in Bale's aerie cavern. Her heart slammed against her ribs in a steady rhythm: *Rave, Rave, Rave.*

Anjali elbowed in front of her. "She has a connection to the dragons. That's valuable to Ashcraft. Considering your colossal failure, Antonio, you're going to need to bring him back something, so I suggest you keep her alive."

Piper wasn't sure if she was supposed to be grateful, but when Anjali tugged on her arm, she got out of the limo.

The jet's engines were already running—was that even safe, *ah mierda*, that so didn't matter right now— and their ragtag group headed for the stairs. Gun-guy, a.k.a. Antonio apparently, had handed Esme to the driver, and he brought up the rear, said gun still in his hand.

He narrowed his eyes at Piper when she glanced back, so she started up the stairs.

Rave, Rave, Rave.

As they settled in under gun-guy's wary eye, Anjali leaned toward Piper.

"I'm sorry," she whispered. "Let me do the talking."

That had always been their way: Anjali talking, Esme paying, Piper tagging along. And it looked like that was never going to stop. Dammit.

"Rave would've saved us," she told Anj. "You didn't have to do this."

"He couldn't even save himself," Anjali shot back. "And when Ashcraft deigns to do his own dirty work, none of them stand a chance."

"The house always wins." Piper held that belief close to her chest. She had to.

But Anj shook her head. "Not when the only deck is stacked by a warlock."

Oh geez. Of all the things she didn't want to hear...

The jet spun, heading for the runway. They'd have at least two more transfers: getting off the plane and getting to Ashcraft. Surely there'd be another chance to escape, to make her way back to Rave.

The engines cranked up another notch as they started to accelerate. Antonio had taken her phone in the limo, but Esme's lost phone was somewhere around her. Maybe she could still call Rave the normal way.

Rave, Rave, Rave!

Outside the plane windows, the lights of the airfield dropped away. The pressure forced Piper back in her seat, but the thought of losing Rave flattened her more.

He was a dragon. Impossible to believe.

And he'd wanted her.

Even more impossible to believe.

But she did, and she needed to tell him she wanted to be his solarys, whatever that meant, whatever other secrets he might be keeping. She put her hand over the cold plexiglass, staring out at the night.

"You are my treasure, Rave," she murmured. "I won't lose you."

Something flashed by the window, too quick to see, and she flinched away. "What the—"

A terrible noise—the shriek of metal tearing—drowned her out. Antonio half rose from his seat, his gaze fixed ahead on the cockpit.

And was cast sideways into the bulkhead when the jet tilted drunkenly.

The engines screamed, and the plane tipped to the other side, as if it was being batted around by a cat. A huge, flying...

Dragon!

Piper grabbed the edges of her chair as the plane skidded in the air and pressed herself to the window.

There! The steady pulse of the jet's position lights illuminated a sleek, powerful shape. She couldn't see it all in the darkness, but a segmented leathery wing stroked past the window, dangerously close to the engine.

If it was sucked in, they'd all fall.

The dragon bumped the jet again, then pounced, forcing the jet's nose downward.

Piper had glimpsed the area just beyond the airfield when they'd flown in.

It was all mountains, jagged and dark and wild.

The jet slalomed again. This time, Antonio landed almost in her lap.

He angled the gun to the window and fired.

Her scream was lost in the sudden howl of wind and

the ringing in her ear. Her whipping hair blinded her.

The gun blasted again, but even through the deafening cacophony she heard the roar of the dragon.

Fury blasted through her veins like lightning and she slammed Antonio toward the window.

It was too small to shove him through—unfortunately—but she coiled herself against the back of her chair and braced hard to kick at his arm. Pinned to the broken shards of plexiglass, he yowled.

He wrenched away from her.

And dropped the gun.

Half falling out of her chair as she was, she slithered the rest of the way to the floor and scuffled for the weapon.

Antonio slammed his boots near her fingers, forcing her to recoil, but then he staggered back, eyes wide.

The third eye in his forehead wept a thin stream of blood, and then he dropped.

Anjali swung the gun toward the other man, but he was still in his seat, jaw slack.

Piper bolted for the cockpit.

The pilot was wrestling the stick, trying to force the jet higher, chanting curse words in his fear.

Her own fear gave her strength as she hauled him out of his seat. He squawked but backed away slowly when he saw Anjali.

Piper threw herself into the still warm seat. Though aerial application had increased her father's pesticide exposure, she'd learned something along the way.

The jet was much, much nicer than the old crop

duster she'd flown, but it only took her a second to ease the plane into a descent. The dragon must have sensed their capitulation, since the buffeting had stopped, but she didn't have time to look for the intriguing shape. She found the landing lights and flicked them on, bathing the foothills in a harsh glow.

They were going down too sharply, and the ground was too rough even for a sturdy farm plane. The sleek jet would break apart on impact.

A longing for Rave shattered inside her, and she hazarded one glance upward through the cockpit's slanting window.

A scintillating jeweled eye stared back.

The shiver down her spine this time wasn't fear, but something joyful and primal. Her heart soared even as she guided the jet lower. The plane bumped lightly in the air, and the stick wriggled in her hand—she'd lost pitch and roll.

The dragon had them in its talons.

"Buckle up," she told Anjali.

She braced herself, but they landed in one piece if not quite feather-light.

After killing the engines, she raced for the door, deploying the steps. From her elevated position, she glimpsed the airfield lights in the distance. The lights of the city limits farther away gleamed on the low clouds. She jumped down and hit the ground running. Rocks and scrub brush threatened to turn her ankle and would have yanked the jet to a crashing halt if not for the dragon's control.

Where was he? Where was—

She whirled to face the jet.

The plane's landing and position lights cast puddles of light in the darkness. Backlit against the glow, perched on the fuselage, was the dragon, vast wings still spread and creating their own glimmering shadow against the night.

The lights glinted on edged scales and a fringe of spikes that crested the serpentine neck and snaked down the lashing tail.

"Rave," she whispered.

The dragon reared up onto his haunches and roared, a sound like a panther, a hawk, and an F-16 rolled into one. One backwash of the leathery wings set her on her heels with a rush of metal-scented air.

Wicked claws screeched down the steel and pierced the cockpit window with a crash, crushing the heavy steel support beam between the plexiglass shield.

The deadly predator subduing its prey.

She took a step forward, her pulse pounding with awe.

Another squeal—of tires this time—made her spin around again.

She recognized the old SUV bouncing across the dirt. Torch and another man were on the ground even faster than she was.

They didn't bother gaping at the dragon.

Torch gave her a nod as they bounded up the jet stairs. If the oily black smoke had hurt him, he seemed to have shaken it off. If anything, he seemed *too* energized, as if the fight was exactly what he'd wanted. That did not bode well for Ashcraft's minions...

In moments they returned. Torch gripped Anjali's arm, almost shoving her down the stairs. Her mouth was a straight, blanched line of shock and dismay. Torch's companion was infinitely more gentle with the lolling Esme. The pilot and the man with the crooked arm hustled down behind them.

Antonio's body was left behind.

The instant they cleared the doorway, the dragon launched skyward with one mighty downbeat of its wings.

Piper had watched raptors over the fields where her father worked and in her own fieldwork, and she'd always admired their keen, relentless power and wild beauty.

Rave inspired all that plus a mythological wonderment that left her unable to look away.

Even when he dove with shocking speed and crushed the nose of the jet into the ground.

The scream of crushed metal was agonizing, and the whole party backed away.

Except Piper. Torch's friend had to drag her back.

She understood why when Rave rocketed up again and then paused, hovering over the wreckage with an incredible display of strength. The gusts of air sent them all back another few steps.

And then he opened his great jaws.

The rush of the fireball was an instant, searing inferno. The jet was engulfed.

"Farther back," Torch warned. "Rave can take it when it blows, but we can't."

His friend tucked Esme into one of the seats of the SUV. Torch ziptied Anjali's hands and all but tossed her into the back. Piper bit her lip as she met Anj's shocked gaze before Torch slammed the door.

There was more to that story, she knew, but it was a mystery for another day.

The pilot and the broken-armed man hovered indecisively, eyes shuttling from the burning wreckage to the SUV to the foothills beyond.

Torch snorted. "I suggest you come up with a good excuse for Ashcraft. Although you'd probably be better off jumping into that fire. Or you can let Ashcraft find a way to explain the tragic crash of his private jet while you run far, far away."

They took the last option, the pilot quickly outdistancing his injured companion.

Torch eyed Piper. "You gonna freak out now?"

"Have I yet?" she countered.

He snorted again, more gently this time. "Rave never believed in true mates."

She gave him a lopsided grin. "And I never believed in dragons."

"Then you two are perfect together."

They weren't perfect at all. They were only...well, human and dragon. They'd both worked so hard for others, they'd all but forgotten themselves. Now they had something that was just theirs. Something rare and precious.

Something magical.

She gazed up at the beautiful beast hovering in the night sky.

"Rave will take you back to the Keep," Torch said.

She barely heard him, or the SUV pulling away. All her senses yearned for the dragon, for Rave.

He touched down delicately in front of her just as the plane exploded. Heat and light radiated around his spread wings, but only a mildly warm breeze brushed back her hair.

She took a step toward him. Now she knew where those chest and arm muscles came from...

He peered down at her, a touch of the wild animal in his wary gaze. He huffed, and a curl of smoke drifted up from his narrow muzzle.

"You don't scare me," she murmured. "You came to save me. You held the plane when I was landing it, didn't you? I was coming back to you. I swear I had nothing to do with Ashcraft's plans, or Anjali's. Do you believe me?"

Slowly he twisted his long neck to bring his triangular head to her level. His glinting eye studied her. The pupil—slit like a cat's—widened, and she saw herself reflected. She didn't look like herself; she looked...wild, free.

Like the true mate of a dragon.

She lifted her hand to his muzzle. The scales were hot, but almost velvety smooth. Though overall dark, each scale at its edges had an opalescent rainbow sheen—the ichor—like a jeweled treasure hidden in the shadows.

"You aren't hidden anymore," she said. "I found you."

He ducked his great head under her hand, almost as if...

Rather than waiting for her doubts to sink her, she ran her fingers down the crest of spines. The spines thickened along his neck and back, but over his wing joints, there was a bare spot.

Just big enough for a certain curvy booty...

He ducked his shoulder, his bent foreleg making a nice stair step.

And then she was riding a dragon.

She wrapped her arms around his neck as he tensed and sprang into the sky.

Her strong legs clamped under the flex of his flight muscles.

Oh man...

The foothills fell away beneath them, the burning jet nothing more than a distant warning.

Despite the cold, desert night and the wind in her face, Piper glowed with warmth. Partly from the hot dragon between her legs, but also from a thrilling joy.

This pure, life-sustaining clarity was what she sought when she looked through her microscope at a drop of water. And here she'd found it, in flames and the night sky, aloft on dragon's wings.

Rave took a wide, looping turn, so easy she didn't fear falling off. But if she did, she had no doubt he'd catch her.

It was a good thing she was so confident, because when the lights of the city gleamed just beyond his outstretched muzzle, he started arrowing downward.

She recognized the medieval turrets of the Keep— now the design aesthetic made sense, as did the remote position on the edge of town—and when they were directly over the middle, Rave folded his wings and dove.

She laughed aloud as they descended in a tight spiral into the well of the secret garden.

Rave landed near the pool, so gently the water barely rippled and she didn't even realize they'd come down. But then the huge body beneath her shimmered with the opalescent energy of the ichor as he changed.

Before she could react, he was twisting to take her in his arms.

For a moment, the vast wings still flowed from his human shoulders, but then he was the man who'd first captured her imagination.

Now she knew he'd never let it go.

Not that there was much left to her imagination. Since he was utterly naked.

"That's convenient," she murmured.

His thickening cock nudged her thigh. "When you laughed, I knew," he said. "I knew you were mine. Not just my solarys, not just my treasure, but my dragon's mate. My heart."

He cupped his hands under her chin, tilting her head up to take her mouth in a wild kiss. Tongues tangled, and their breaths turned to gasps. He stripped her bare in a heartbeat, his hands claiming every inch of her.

She did the same, finding taut muscle and smooth skin where wings and spikes had been.

"You're glorious," she murmured. "So strong. So beautiful."

"So yours."

His growl vibrated through her, weakening her knees and sending a burst of hot, wet need through her core.

She ran her hands over the map of his treasure. "You're really okay? When that black smoke hit you..." She looked up at him when he clasped her hands together. "You know I wanted no part of that, right?"

"I know." His gaze glittered down at her. The pupils slitted, revealing more of the stormy blue-gray. "If you want my ichor, you have only to ask."

He dropped to his knees in front of her, his hands trailing down to her hips. "You are my solarys. The light and the heat of my dragon. The heart of my treasure. My life. How I won you when I never believed such a one as you existed..." He shook his head, then leaned forward to press a kiss to her navel. "You are the flame within me now."

She feathered her fingers through his hair so he looked up at her. "I want you inside me."

He took her hard and fast and she welcomed him with equal intensity. The fear and shock that had left her heart pounding before turned to passion, flaming through her blood.

She screamed when she came and his roar echoed her.

When they floated in the pool afterward, she touched her mouth. Her lips were swollen and tender, but only from kisses.

"It's the mate bond. Through it, I can share some of the healing power of the ichor with you, just as you were able to call to me." He kissed her wet hair. "Who hit you?"

She snuggled against his chest. "He's dead." She should be more horrified by that, she knew, but they would have killed Rave. Maybe some of the dragon's unblinking ferocity was in her now, borne on the mate bond.

His arm tightened possessively. "I would kill him again for you."

"It's over."

She knew it wasn't, but she would hold onto the illusion, just for a little bit.

Rave seemed inclined to agree. "I need to get a bed down here."

"You have a lovely bed in your suite. The garden is perfect just like it is."

He huffed out a breath. "You're right. We can use the bed upstairs when we are being civilized."

She turned in the circle of his arms to float over him. "I like you wild."

He ran his hands down her back to squeeze her ass. "That delights me since I want to show you some very wild things."

"More secrets revealed." Dipping her head, she kissed the bare skin above his heart.

Though he didn't move beyond a satisfied sigh, a shockwave moved through the water, sending ripples bouncing back at them. Each little wave was topped with sparkling rainbows.

His eyebrows rose. "What was that?"

She looked down. "Rave," she gasped.

Where she'd kissed him, a stylized sun burned in his skin, its rays spiraling across his pectoral muscle. After a heartbeat, it faded to the half-hidden metallic gleam of the rest of his markings. The water settled with one last stray gleam like a shooting star.

"Hmm, see?" he said smugly. "I am yours."

Rising up to balance her forearms on his broad chest, she sputtered. "What... How..."

"You claimed the dragon. It sings for you, burning through my hide. My solarys, marked on my skin."

Tentatively, she traced the new lines. "Does it hurt?"

"Only the thought that I might have lost you." His deep inhalation floated them both higher in the water. "We thought we would keep you locked up down here at the center of our hoard."

"Oh really?" She dug the points of her elbows into his ribs.

He winced. "Really. But now I understand that's a terrible idea."

"Good thing," she said wryly.

"His solarys is a dragon's breath and fire. I could no more hide you away than the dragon. You are both meant to shine." He rolled her in the water, anchoring his hips between her legs. "Now confess. You have no reservations about loving a dragon-shifter?"

She widened her eyes at him. "Loving a rich, sexy, smart, and powerful man who turns into a beast in bed even when there's no bed *and* can fly me to the stars? I think I won the jackpot."

"You think?" he growled.

She wriggled against him, centering his bulging length at her center. "Well, it might've been pure dumb luck."

"You can roll my dice as many times as you want," he said. "But you've already won it all: my treasure, my heart. My love."

About the Author

Elsa Jade—also scribbling as Jessa Slade—writes sexy shapeshifter stories and other tales of paranormal romance as well as urban fantasy romance and science fiction romance.

You can find her online at:
ElsaJade.com
JessaSlade.com

While you are there, sign up for her *New Release & Sales Alert* newsletter to get the latest book news.

THANK YOU!

Thank you for reading! I'm so glad you're along on this shapeshifting adventure with me. If you enjoyed the story, I hope you'll tell your book-loving friends on social media, with a review, or through word of mouth so we can add more fans to our nefarious plans for conquering the world with stories of sexy shapeshifters and bold heroines. Thank you for *being* a reader!

Printed in Great Britain
by Amazon

59239049R00119